The Expurgator

The Expurgator

ANDREW YORK

PUBLISHED FOR THE CRIME CLUB BY

DOUBLEDAY & COMPANY, INC.

GARDEN CITY, NEW YORK

1973

The characters and events in this novel
are invented, as is the village of Dort.
Any resemblance to real characters or events
is coincidental and unintended.

ISBN: 0-385-02241-7
Library of Congress Catalog Card Number 72–84955
Copyright © 1972 by Christopher Nicole
Printed in the United States of America

Contents

"How fast has brother followed brother,
From sunshine to the sunless land!"

William Wordsworth

PART ONE

THE SUNSHINE

1

THE woman switched off the ignition, allowed the car to coast to a halt, the wheels to brush the kerb. She left her hands on the wheel, slowly filled her lungs with air. Her palms were damp with sweat, inside her gloves. She had thin hands, matching the rest of her; she was not tall, and the wisp of figure allowed her to look like a young boy, when, as now, she wore her midnight blue trouser suit. Her face was serious, with a long nose and pointed chin. Her eyes were a thoughtful amber. Only the headscarf which concealed her hair, and shrouded her ears and cheeks, was entirely feminine.

Her scarf, and her anxiety. She glanced at the man. 'This is a nice car.' Her voice was low.

'You say that about every car.' The man's voice was flat, accentless. He moved the rear-view mirror, adjusted his tie, tilted his soft hat to a very fine angle, gave his gloves a little jerk up each wrist. 'It's time.'

He opened the door, stepped out. It was a dull December night, dampened by a light mist which contained a hint of drizzle. The man turned up his coat collar. The woman stood beside him, half his size, buttoning her leather carcoat, looking up and down the street. The Surrey town was quiet, already darkened, every window a gleam of light behind the drawn curtains; it was the pause between the return of the young children from preparatory school, and the arrival of their fathers from London. In each sitting room, tea was being served and consumed; jam was being spread and smeared, and spilt on freshly laundered tablecloths and already grubby blouses. Wives were hurrying upstairs to freshen lipstick, and, depending upon their husbands' tastes, were putting fresh pots of tea on to draw, or slipping something alcoholic into the cocktail shaker. And in so ordered and unchanging a community, there was not even a beat policeman to be seen; a Panda Car patrol every two hours was considered sufficient, and the last one had droned up the street just fifteen minutes earlier.

The man and the woman walked together, heels clicking on the pavement. One or two of the curtains moved, and then slid back again. It wasn't Dad coming home early; visitors for the St. Johns. No, for the Walners, apparently. From America, perhaps.

The man pushed open the gate, walked up the stone path, the woman now a little behind him. At the three little steps he paused, glanced over his shoulder at the heavily pruned stalks which filled the peat-covered beds on either side. 'Roses,' he said. 'The man is civilised.' He felt in his coat pocket, took out two masks, gave the woman hers. They were enlarged dominoes, fitted neatly over nose and around eyes, and then protruded downwards and outwards in an apron which shaded mouth and chin but did not interfere with speech. Standing in the porch, the two people were hidden from the street.

The man rang the bell. And again. The door opened, and a small girl with yellow pigtails stared at them. 'Yes?' Her half-smile faded into a half-frown. 'What do you want?' she asked, a note of alarm clouding her American accent. 'You're . . .'

'Masked,' the man agreed. 'It's all a game. We're friends of your daddy's.' While she spoke he gently pushed her into the house, and at the same moment took a small Browning automatic pistol from his pocket. 'Now you mustn't make a sound. Where's Mummy?'

The child goggled at him.

'You're Ann,' the woman said. 'A pretty name, Ann. Where's Mummy, Ann?'

Ann pointed to the door on the left. 'It's tea-time,' she explained.

'I'd love a cuppa.' The woman opened the door.

Jane Walner turned. She had been bending over the table, placing a fresh plateful of scones. She frowned, and then straightened, watched her daughter come in, followed by the man and the woman; the woman closed the door. 'What on earth are you doing, Ann?' Jane Walner was a Californian. 'Who are these people?'

'Friends of Daddy's. Playing a game,' Ann said.

'But they're masked!' The boy had hastily swallowed a piece of cake. He was somewhat older than his sister, had the same fair hair. Not, apparently, inherited from their mother, who was dark.

'All part of the game, Paul,' the man assured him. 'Would you sit down, Mrs. Walner? On the settee. You too, Paul. And you, Ann.'

'But . . .' Jane Walner said.

'Just a game, Mrs. Walner,' the woman insisted. 'Just a game. Do please remember that.' She glanced down at the little girl standing in front of her, and Jane Walner swallowed, inhaled, licked her lips, and sat down. Fear did not fit her face; she had sensible, blunt features, a trim, solid figure. Her hair had been recently set; there was just a trace of grey amongst the brown. Her dress might have come off a peg at Harrods.

'Would you sit with your mother?' the woman invited, as the two children hesitated.

Jane Walner licked her lips once again. 'It's all part of the game, Paul,' she said. 'Do play it properly.'

'The maid?' the man asked.

'Thursday is her afternoon off,' Jane Walner said.

'That checks,' the woman agreed.

'But I'll take a look.' The man turned his hand upwards, so that the little Browning was clearly visible. 'Know anything about guns, Paul?'

'Oh, yes,' Paul said. 'That looks like the Browning point six three five calibre. The one they call the Baby. Is it real?'

'Ten out of ten,' the man said. 'So you know that it's

absolutely silent, well, to all intents and purposes. And yet it can kill. We have two.'

The woman showed them her gun.

The man closed the door behind him, walked down the hall, opened other doors, looked into the kitchen, went down to the cellar. Then he went upstairs, checked the three bedrooms, the two bathrooms. Solid, middle-class comfort and respectability. He thought Walner must enjoy living like this, even if his wife might compare it unfavourably with her home in Sacramento. Walner had done well. Not as well as might once have been expected. But then, a man must choose. And having chosen he must abide by his choice. And its consequences. Not only a man like Kevin Walner.

The man sighed, paused in front of the bathroom mirror to make a small adjustment to his already tight and neatly centred tie knot, went back downstairs. 'I like your house,' he told Jane Walner. 'Much ground?'

'Not quite an acre.' Her breathing had settled down.

'Trees?' The man took a long length of nylon line from his pocket.

'Apples. Four. And a little greenhouse with grapes. What are you doing?'

'All part of the game,' the man assured her. 'Now just relax, Mrs. Walner, and nobody is going to get hurt. We don't even want you to be uncomfortable. What about switching on the box? Children's television, isn't it? You'll enjoy that, eh, Ann?' He knelt in front of her, expertly secured her ankles together, then carried the rope along to her mother.

'An adventure serial,' the woman said, adjusting the dials. 'I do like adventure serials.' She poured herself a cup of tea. 'Mrs. Walner?' Jane Walner shook her head. 'Not yet a habit?' the woman asked. 'Just being English, for the kids' sake?' But she was less composed than she seemed; the cup rattled in the saucer. She put it down, wandered around the room, touching ornaments, lingering over a cut-glass decanter. Then she sat in a straight chair, a little behind the settee, so that the Walners had to turn their heads to see her. The pistol remained in her hand.

'Is this necessary?' Jane Walner asked as her ankles were drawn together.

The man carried the rope from her to Paul. 'I don't really think I could ask for your word, Mrs. Walner. If I gave my word in these circumstances, I'd certainly break it the moment I could.'

'But what do you want?' Jane Walner asked. 'My husband will be home any minute.' She bit her lip.

'As you say, Mrs. Walner.' The man stretched the rope upwards, made Paul lean forward, secured his wrists behind him. 'This is a nuisance, but so long as you all sit still and relax, you shouldn't be uncomfortable. And I'll make you a promise; one hour after we leave, I'll ring the police and have them come around and let you out. Okay?'

She gazed at him, trying to reconcile his manner, the softness of his voice, his apparent anxiety to make things as easy as possible for them, with what he was actually doing. She thought, perhaps it *is* all a game, after all. A vast practical joke.

The man tied Ann's wrists, carried the still lengthy line over the back of the settee and round each leg, secured it at floor level, drawn tight. 'Good,' he said. 'Now, I have to gag you as well. There's the part I really don't like. First, would anyone like something to drink?'

Ann Walner nodded, her head jerking up and down while she gazed at the masked face.

'Milk?' The man poured from the jug on the table, held the glass to her lips. 'Paul? No? Mrs. Walner? Well, as I said, it'll only be an hour. Open wide.' There were three pear-shaped wooden plugs, each consisting of two jaws separated by a small spring. The man squeezed one shut, inserted it into Paul's mouth, released the spring so that the expanding plug forced the boy's jaws apart. Then he did the same for Jane Walner and her daughter. 'Now, there's nothing to be scared of,' he said. 'You couldn't choke on those if you tried, and you'll find the wood will keep moisture in your mouths. Okay?'

They gazed at him.

'Cars,' the woman said.

The man looked at his watch. 'Time,' he agreed. He opened the door, went into the hall. He leaned against the wall, the pistol once again in his hand. He listened to the cars, drifting up the street. For half an hour the village would be alive again, then it would slumber once more. People would settle down in front of their television sets, would go out to bridge, would sit and chat. People.

He listened to an engine, closer at hand, its beat changing as it entered a garage. He never moved, and there was no change in his rate of breathing. He listened to heels clicking on the stone drive, to the scrape of a key in the latch. He watched the door open, swing towards him, and then swing away from him to bank shut. He stepped forward, drove the muzzle of the pistol into Kevin Walner's back. 'Don't make a sound,' he said.

Walner's back tensed, and then relaxed. There were different ways to treat different people; Walner was not the sort of man to panic. His features were even more blunt than his wife's, his build even stockier. His suit was bespoke, but not, the man thought, from Savile Row. His tie was silk, though, and his topcoat was new. 'Who are you?' he asked, his head only half turned. There was the slightest trace of a foreign accent in his voice, but he did not sound afraid.

'We've never met, Mr. Walner. I've an invitation for you to go visiting.'

'My family?'

The man moved away, opened the living room door. Walner stood there for a moment. 'They are not hurt?'

'You tell him, Mrs. Walner,' the man suggested.

Jane Walner's head moved to and fro.

'And they won't be, if everyone keeps his and her head,'

the man promised. 'You're going to come with us, Mr. Walner.'

'Where?'

'I'll tell you that when we're in the car. But I have given your wife my word that I'll ring the police an hour after we leave here, and tell them what has happened.'

'Then you are a fool,' Walner said. 'Do you expect me to believe that?'

'Mr. Walner,' the man said. 'I am *asking* you to believe that. Because that way, no one gets hurt.'

Walner looked at him, frowning. '*No* one?'

'That's what I said. So let's go. The hour begins when we leave here.'

Walner gazed at his family once again, and then shrugged. 'We shall have to trust him, my dear. Whatever they want, they will not get it from me.' He glanced at the man. 'You are wasting your time, you know.'

'I'm almost inclined to agree with you.' The man shrugged in turn. 'But I just carry out instructions. Let's go.'

Walner hesitated, then he stepped forward, kissed his wife on her forehead, and turned to the door. The woman got up.

'You're going to be in all the newspapers. Isn't that exciting?' She closed the living room door, opened the front door in turn. The only sound was the voice from the television. The woman took off her mask, and the man handed her his. Walner gazed from one to the other, memorising their faces.

'Now,' the man said. 'If you try anything foolish, I will shoot you, Mr. Walner. And having done that, as to anyone looking on, should there be anyone, you will just stagger and collapse as if you had had a heart attack, we shall of course bring you back here, and we shall then shoot your wife and children. Please believe me.'

Walner continued to gaze at him. 'I believe you would,' he said.

The woman went out first, walked down the path, opened the garage. Walner followed, with the man at his elbow.

'Give her your keys,' the man said.

Walner hesitated, then dug his hand into his trouser pocket, handed the woman the keys. She opened the back door of the car and Walner got in. The man sat beside him. The woman got into the front seat, started the engine. The car reversed out of the garage.

'Now, perhaps you can tell me where we are going.' Walner leaned back, looked through the window.

'Into London,' the man said.

Walner glanced at him. 'At this hour? You seem to be a very confident man.'

'I take precautions,' the man said. 'For instance, I would like to give you an injection. There will be no pain. Not even any discomfort, I promise you that. But it is obviously essential that you do not see where we are going, and the only alternative is a bump on the head. That would be painful.'

'You are a most remarkable fellow,' Walner said. 'You know, when one reads the newspapers or watches the television every day, one almost expects to be kidnapped. Almost. One sees it as a possibility. I always assumed that it was going to be a *most* unpleasant experience.'

'Life is sufficiently unpleasant, without adding to it,' the man said. 'Would you like a drink, first? There is some brandy.'

The woman reached into her coat pocket, handed the flask into the back seat.

Walner balanced it in his hand. 'Yes,' he said at last. 'I think perhaps I would like a drink. If it will not react with the injection.'

'It may help it to take a little faster,' the man said. 'But that is all to the good.'

'And it will leave no ill effects?' Walner asked.

'You will never know you had it,' the man promised.

'Time.' The woman pulled off the road on to a deserted layby.

'I would not like to make a mistake, you see,' the man explained. 'I would not like you to lose your nerve at the last moment, and start struggling, either.'

The car stopped, the woman turned round and knelt on the seat, facing them, her pistol in her hand.

'You are very efficient.' Walner took a long drink of brandy, corked the flask. 'You are delivering me to an address in London. Will the people who are waiting for me be as pleasant?'

'Now that I cannot say,' the man said. 'But I would be confident, if I were you. Your sleeve.'

Walner hesitated once again, and then pushed his jacket sleeve up his arm, released his cufflink and bared his forearm. The woman switched on a pocket torch, shone it on the white flesh. The man took a small bottle from his pocket, a large piece of cotton wool. He poured antiseptic liquid on to the cotton wool, stroked Walner's forearm, replaced bottle and the cotton wool, took a hypodermic needle from a plastic case. He placed two fingers on the flesh, and drove the needle in. He waited for a few seconds, withdrew the needle, and returned it to its case. The woman switched off the flashlight.

'That was very well done,' Walner said. 'You should be practising medicine. Or are you a junkie?'

'I don't even smoke,' the man said. 'Now, that thing will take a few minutes to work; is there anything you'd like to do with the time? I'm afraid we can't let you out of the car, but would you like a cigarette? Another drink?'

Walner shook his head.

'Maybe you have other tastes,' the man said. 'Would you like to kiss the lady? She is a very pretty girl. I'm afraid there isn't really time for anything more than that.'

Walner looked at the woman, who continued to kneel on the front seat, staring at him. Her expression had not changed. 'Why should I wish to do that?'

'Who knows,' the man said.

'You are a very odd pair,' Walner said. 'These people to whom I am going, do they wish something from me? Something to do with my work? Or am I to be used as some sort of a hostage?'

'I told you, they don't give me the details,' the man said.

Walner sighed, and frowned. 'Perhaps I should not have had the brandy,' he said. 'For a moment there I felt distinctly odd. I do not suppose I'm important enough to be a hostage. But I have nothing to tell anyone, either. Nothing at all. That is the set-up, the way the thing is being done. Nobody knows anything, except his own little niche. What's on his desk before him.' He sighed again. 'This injection is making me feel very strange. My heartbeat feels different.'

'I imagine it *is* the brandy,' the man explained. 'Nothing to worry about.'

Walner sighed for a third time. 'Yes,' he said. 'The brandy.' He gazed at the woman; her face was a faint glimmer of light from the street lamp. 'You are right, you know,' he said. 'She is an extremely pretty girl. Is she going to be my gaoler?'

'I doubt it,' the man said. 'If you want something from her, you had better take it now.'

Walner sat up, reached for breath. 'And you, young lady, you do exactly what you are told?'

'Most of the time.' There was sweat on her face. On a cold December afternoon? Walner reached out his hand, and stroked her cheek, let his fingers go round the back of her neck, gave a little gasp, and sat back. His eyes remained open, staring at the girl.

'We can go now,' the man said.

The woman turned round, put the car into gear, pulled on to the road. The surface was wet, and for a moment they skidded before she got the nose straight again.

'Easy.' The man held Walner's wrist, gazed at the watch. 'You were nervous, tonight.'

'I thought he *was* going to kiss me,' she said.

'It would be a good way to die,' the man said. 'In the act of kissing a pretty girl. You were nervous even before we reached the house.'

'Yes.' She stared into the twin beams of light cast by the headlamps. 'I was nervous. Because of the house. I much prefer the other way. I hope there will be no more, like this.'

The man folded Walner's hands on his lap, reached up and closed his eyes. 'He died happy. It is very important, to die happy. I do not like the thought of your being nervous. Whatever the immediate reason, it is a sign of tension, of decline. You must always remember poor Peter. I do not think, when he died, that *he* was happy.'

2

WILDE leaned on the bar. 'I will have a Bacardi and coca-cola,' he said. 'With a great deal of ice. But no lemon, please.'

'One Bacardi and coke, coming up,' agreed the barman. 'Guest in the hotel, are you, sir?'

"Just arrived,' Wilde said. 'Hong Kong, don't you know.' He glanced at his watch. 'Now I am waiting for my wife, as usual.' He smiled. When he smiled, he became almost hand-some. In repose his face was gaunt, with high cheekbones and mild, light blue eyes. His dark brown hair receded, lay smoothly. He allowed himself sideboards, but otherwise his cut was old-fashioned. So was his suit, dark grey, Italian made. It fitted his six foot two inches of height as if sculpted into place, tapering from wide shoulders to hips which were unusually slender in a man who clearly would not see forty again. He looked tired, but there were tremendous reserves of energy in his every movement, even the way in which he picked up his glass.

'On business, are you, sir?' asked the barman.

Wilde nodded. 'But not today. We've been flying all night. I think I shall go to bed. Whenever my wife chooses to arrive.' He gazed into the hotel lobby, finished his drink, stood up. 'Put that on my bill, will you?'

He walked across the carpeted floor, moving without sound. He had entered that noiselessly, too, the barman remembered. It was his most remarkable feature, the silence of his movements, the air of quiet which surrounded him.

'Do you know,' Wilde said, 'I thought you had got yourself lost.'

The woman turned, her mouth opening. She was tall, only a few inches shorter than Wilde himself, and her flame red maxicoat made her appear more slender than she actually was. Her hair was jet, and parted in the centre; it descended to each shoulder in lacquered perfection. Her face was calm. Even now, when she was clearly terrified, her emotion was obvious only to him. It was a beautiful face; at first glance it seemed to be dominated by the straight nose, the wide mouth, the rounded chin, and then these luxuries faded into insignificance as the eyes were reached. Even Wilde was always forgetting how wide set were her eyes; he had never seen them matched. And how clear the green; it was like looking through tinted glass, but not at a view. Catherine's eyes were eternity.

He kissed her mouth before she could close it again, allowed their tongues to brush. She had also required fortification. Gin, he decided.

'Jonas,' she whispered. 'You are mad. Mad. Quite . . .'

'My wife has arrived,' Wilde said. 'I think we shall go up to our room, now. And we won't be down for lunch. Will you send a menu, please?'

'Of course, Mr. Williams.' The manager allowed his glance to drift down Catherine's arms as she took off her gloves. He was conditioned to suspicion; her suntan was not quite as fresh as her husband's, and that had been an unusually warm welcome for a wife who presumably had been squirm-

ing in the next seat all night on the flight from Hong
Kong. Apparently she had gone straight from the airport to
a hairdresser; no woman had ever looked like this immediately after a long journey. On the other hand, she was
obviously not less than ten years younger than her husband,
and she did wear a wedding ring, and there was a great
deal of money knocking around, judging by her clothes. A
second wife, perhaps, for a doting, successful businessman.
The manager snapped his fingers, and a uniformed bellhop
hurried forward.

'Mr. and Mrs. Williams. Number Seventeen. It's on the
first floor, Mr. Williams, overlooking the square. One of our
best suites. I'm sure you'll like it.'

Catherine entered the lift as if it were the gas chamber,
stood with her back to the doors. Wilde was at her shoulder.
'Did you get what you wanted?'

Her head half turned, and then straightened again. 'Oh,
yes,' she said. 'Oh, yes.'

The lift halted, the doors opened. The bellhop led them
along a deep carpeted corridor. Wilde slipped his hand into
hers. 'When is your appointment?'

She glanced at him. 'I should have one in five minutes.
But . . .'

'You'll skip that one. Bed is what we want. And need.
Wouldn't you say?'

There was colour in her cheeks.

The bellhop opened the door, stood aside. 'Your bags came
up earlier, Mr. Williams.'

'Thank you.' Wilde slipped a fifty-pence piece into the
boy's hand, closed the door. Catherine had walked across
the room to the window, gazed through the net curtains.

She turned, slowly. 'I nearly didn't come.'

'Green-eyed girls are always fickle.' He knelt in front of
the fridge, took out the bucket and the bottle of champagne.

'Is it our honeymoon?' She opened the bedroom door,
looked inside, closed it again.

There was a faint pop as Wilde removed the cork. 'We

just love each other, darling.' He poured. 'How long have I got?'

She stood beside him. 'No time at all, Jonas. Don't you understand? Less than ever, now. That number hasn't been used in eight months.'

'But his nibs, being a civil servant at heart, would not have it disconnected. I was quite surprised when it actually rang; I only tried it on spec.' He brushed his glass against hers. 'Why did you answer it?'

'Because . . .' She drained her glass, set it on the table. 'Because maybe I knew that one day it would ring. But don't you see? If I knew that, then *he* knew it too.'

'But you answered it, sweetheart.' Wilde refilled their glasses, unbuttoned her coat. 'And having done that, you came along here. I'll make you a promise; if he divorces you, I'll marry you.'

'You're an absolute riot.' She shrugged her shoulders free of the coat, opened her handbag, lit a cigarette with long, nervous fingers. Her skirt reached farther than the last time he'd seen her, but then, skirts were coming down all over. And her legs were the same slender perfection that he would never forget. Her dress was blue velvet, trimmed with mink at hem and collar and cuffs. He didn't think she'd paid more than a hundred pounds for it; he knew she liked to shop around.

There was a zip, at the back. She stood with her arms folded, one hand holding the champagne glass to her lips. 'I answered it,' she said, half to herself. 'And I came, too. I suppose I'm just as mad. You started something, the last time, you know, Jonas. Something I bet you never expected. I never did, anyway.'

Wilde kissed the nape of her neck, allowed the dress to fall to the ground, moved his hands under her armpits. She was emancipated, and her breasts were always surprising, larger than he had any right to hope, in so slim a frame. And she was still chilled from the air outside. She shivered as he touched her. 'I don't want to know,' he said in her ear.

'But I want you to.' She turned in his arms. 'Only twice, so far. Once out of curiosity, I think. The second time . . . I don't know.'

'Twice in eight months,' he said. 'No wonder you're starving. There's the menu. Will you order?'

'I have supreme confidence in your taste, Jonas. When it comes to food or wine. But make it something light, will you? If you'll excuse the pun.'

He waited for the bedroom door to close, said, 'Come.'

The bellhop kept his eyes on the ceiling; Catherine had forgotten her dress. 'The trout's very good today, sir.'

'Then the trout it shall be. Followed by the veal. And another bottle of the Krug. And I want it in fifteen minutes. We're starving.'

'Yes, sir.' The hall door closed.

Wilde went into the bedroom, Catherine sat on the bed, naked, smoking a cigarette. With hair so perfect she might have been posing for a picture. Woman Thinking. No. Nymph Reflecting. How could thighs so slender, so immature in every sense, belong to other than a nymph? When women interested him, he estimated their potential in terms of colours. At their first meeting, on the Dunkirk waterfront, how many eternities ago, he had selected mist grey, for her. He had been right. It had not been a criticism of her qualities as either woman or mistress, but an estimate of her elusiveness.

He sat beside her. 'How long do I have?'

'I must be home by four.'

'Why?'

'Because Pop will be coming in at five, Jonas.'

He took the cigarette from between her fingers, stubbed it in the ashtray by the bed. 'No, he won't, darling. Not today. I'm meeting him at five-thirty.'

(ii)

He had forgotten her restlessness. It was a residue of passion, and it drove her onwards, even after passion was spent.

She walked, up and down the bedroom, throwing each long leg in front of the other, smoking a cigarette. Lung cancer was a preferable future to nervous exhaustion. Now her hair was untidy. Nothing that a few strokes of a brush could not fix. Now that so flawless complexion was mottled, finger marked in red and white. Nothing that would not fade in an hour. Now she was a woman, not a nymph, and the woman was at rest. But already the tensions, the anxieties, were building up all over again. They would become invisible when she had renewed her make-up, put on her dress. She would walk the streets like a queen, repelling familiarity with a glance. Only two men in the entire world would know the cauldron within. Two?

'What time is it?'

'Four-thirty. Would you like a cup of tea?'

'I'm still digesting that lunch. I don't suppose you have a cap of any sort?'

'You might find something. You can always tilt your chin.'

She hunted through his suitcase, selected a pale blue silk handkerchief, bound up her hair, stepped into the shower. There was the act of finality. For another eight months? Or forever?

She towelled, standing by the bed, scattering water over him. 'Would you have called, if you hadn't been brought to London?'

'I don't know. I've thought of it, several times. But so long as I'm out of England, I'm able to resist the temptation.'

'Will you call again?'

'Will you come again, Cathy?'

She dressed herself, took off his handkerchief, dropped it on the floor. She used his brush on her hair, frowned at herself in the mirror, stuck her tongue between her teeth as she smoothed her eyebrows. 'I came to say goodbye,' she said.

'This morning? Or this afternoon?'

She lipsticked, seemed satisfied. 'This morning.' She sat on the bed beside him. 'Please don't touch, Jonas, not now. Oh, my God, you're bleeding.'

'I think you must file your teeth. I always did think so.'

'I don't suppose you can put plaster, right there. I'm sorry, Jonas. Am I very unlike other women?'

'Yes,' he said. 'Other women all want to be like you. But they seldom make it.'

She got up, walked to the window, lit a fresh cigarette. 'I thought we would have a quiet drink. I even thought we might lunch.'

'We did.'

'And then I thought we'd shake hands, like civilised people, and say how nice it was to meet again, after all these months.'

'I am not a civilised person, thank God. And on the evidence of your dental work, you aren't either.'

'What are you going to do about the room?'

'I shall come back here this evening, after seeing Sir Gerald, and I shall check out. I'll them you've had a bereavement, and we're both rushing off to Cumberland, or somewhere like that. You'll be waiting for me at the station.'

'After seeing Pop.' She slipped her feet into her shoes. 'You are not civilised, Jonas. You are a savage, and you make me into a savage, too. I wish there *was* a jungle, out there. But I can't change the world, or you, or me. I won't ever leave Pop, Jonas. It's more than a marriage. You know that. But now, since you, it's a marriage as well. I'm doubly important, now.'

Wilde said nothing. There was nothing for him to say.

Catherine Light went into the sitting room. He listened to her opening the fridge, close it again. She came back into the bedroom, carrying the ice bucket in both hands. It held only water, now. 'There's no champagne left.' She placed the bucket on his stomach, smiled as he tensed his muscles against the weight and the sudden cold. 'He's taking me to New York in March. The third, to be precise. It's some sort of conference, and we'll be gone a fortnight. But if, after that, you call again, Jonas, I'll come.'

(iii)

It was time to go. Not merely because he had an appointment, but because without her the suite was cheerless. And haunting. She wore Adoration.

Wilde showered, towelled—even the towels still carried her scent—ran his shaver over his chin. As she had said, he was mad. Absolutely bloody mad. Not to telephone. That made sense, in the circumstances. He was mad to have fallen in love, at his age, with Catherine Light. Correction. Lady Catherine Light.

Even had he been a rising executive in some manufacturing firm or other, the circumstances would have been ridiculous, the classic cliché of ambition chasing wealth, grammar school hunting Roedean, city clerk courting Oxford graduate, and now, worst of all, life-long bachelor on the wrong side of forty swinging with the aristocratic wife of his employer. Sunday newspaper stuff.

But he wasn't a rising executive in some manufacturing business or other. He was Jonas Wilde. His job was not new motor cars or ultra-modern furniture. He was a man with no future, whose past did not bear consideration, who existed by reason of one man's use for his talents. And that man was named Gerald Light.

He closed the door behind him, took the elevator to the ground floor. And he had been in love before. He didn't ever want to forget that. He couldn't afford to. So there was no possibility of Catherine being a Russian agent. She had even been involved in this frightening business which was his life, once. But she was returning the love, where

Jocelyn's had been all pretence. That made her as vulnerable as himself.

Vulnerable. There was the operative word, at this moment. Because Cathy was gone, and it was time to be what he was. He paused in the lobby, lit a cigarette. He was deliberately provoking his senses, his instincts, seeking the possibility of trouble where there could not possibly be trouble. The waiting lounge off the lobby contained two elderly ladies, heads close together, exchanging some vital piece of gossip; two Africans, either diplomats or businessmen, expecting a British host for the evening, perhaps, occasionally dropping a remark about the iniquities of British weather; and a man reading a newspaper. Also waiting for a taxi? Newspapers hid a great many faults, but they did not hide legs. And shoes. These were shoes Wilde had seen before. Soft leather, pointed. Old-fashioned shoes. He had seen them at Nice airport, mentally photographed them, without reason, other than that his brain photographed everything gleaned by his eyes, and upon that photography his life had more than once depended.

Suddenly he was sweating. At his own carelessness? Or at having, unwittingly, involved Catherine in this aspect of his life. Catherine was gone. The man was still here. Which meant nothing at all.

He went outside, buttoning his topcoat.

'Taxi, sir?'

'I'll walk, thanks very much.' Which made sense. The hotel was only five minutes from Oxford Street. But there are sufficient little alleys in Mayfair. And it was December, already dark, and cold enough to encourage thoughts of a white Christmas. Wilde walked, hands deep in his pockets. He had been relaxing. As if Wilde could ever afford to relax. Now he could feel the rivers of nervous tension creeping up his spine. Not hatred, yet. No hatred at all, this time. The man behind him was merely doing a job of work, was not a target.

He turned into an already night-shrouded street; there

were only two streetlights, well spaced. It was just on five, and time was running short. He continued to walk purposefully, noiselessly, hands in his pockets, gazing straight in front of him, apparently, scrutinising the buildings that he passed, high, towering over his head, only occasionally lighted. Flats and apartments, for the more successful of London's office population, and these had not yet left their offices.

A deep doorway, in a pool of blackness. Without hesitation or change of stride Wilde sidestepped into the black, turned on the balls of his feet, sucked air into his lungs, counted to five, slowly, and stepped out again.

The man with the pointed shoes halted, his face a picture of consternation, even in the darkness. It took him a tenth of a second to start to move. A tenth of a second too long. Wilde's hands shot out, fingers like steel claws closed on the unprotected throat, and the man was whipped sideways, hurled into the darkness of the doorway, pinned against the old wood, eyes bulging as Wilde squeezed.

The body sagged, and Wilde released the throat. With tremendous speed his fingers rippled down the coat front, releasing buttons, did the same for the jacket. He drove both hands inside, one moving left and the other right. There was no pistol. From the inside breast pocket Wilde removed the wallet. There was nothing else.

The man struck upwards, both hands rising together. Wilde never moved, merely sank his heels, his weight, his shoulders, into the place where he stood. The man's hands struck Wilde's arms, travelling with tremendous force, and fell back again. His mouth fell open as he stared at his assailant. Wilde smiled at him, moved his right arm back, the fist already closed. It covered only six inches, exploded into the unprotected stomach.

Wilde stepped back, pocketed the wallet, turned into the alley. From behind him there came a single retch, and then silence. Oxford Street was only a hundred yards away. Wilde paused under the first street lamp, flipped open the wallet, the card holder inside; people brushed his shoulders, and he ignored them. Then he smiled again. Things were not good. But they were better than they might have been.

Oxford Street was a blaze of light, from every store, from the decorations. It was also a mass of people. Walking was as difficult as swimming against the tide. But it was always interesting. People were the only interesting things in the world, and here was people, *en masse*. Grandfathers and grandmothers, huddled against the cold, clutching their various shopbags and chattering anxiously about the possibility of catching, or missing, this or that bus, this or that underground train; fathers and mothers, clutching their various children, muttering anxiously about having spent a pound or two more than they had intended; lovers, clutching each other, dreaming their way to the next crisis; and the children themselves, clutching the placebos they had been bought to keep them quiet while the real business of filling Father Christmas's sledge went on around them, shivering and chattering, and yawning, dreaming of television, and bed. Christmas was a family occasion, and lonely people had no place in it. His place was on board the boat, with a bottle of champagne—correction, a case of champagne—and whatever companionship he could collect, for the night. Just the night.

He checked his watch, stood outside Selfridge's, hands deep in his pockets, on the very edge of the kerb, out of the way of the solid masses entering and leaving the famous store, apparently all at once. He suggested one of two alternatives: A man shopping by himself, unable to make up his mind where next to go, or, more probable, a man waiting for his wife, cold and ill-tempered. A man not used to being ill-tempered, despite the granite hardness of his face. But this evening the corners of his mouth turned down, and the light blue eyes were dull.

He studied the cars. They moved by, slowly, inching their ways along the packed street, taxies, buses, big cars, little cars, sports cars, sedan cars, new cars, old cars. Wilde's head never moved. He gazed at numberplate after numberplate. He was obeying instructions, because he always obeyed instructions. He thought it amusing, that he should trust this man so absolutely. He had no alternative. When Gerald Light snapped his fingers, Wilde would be dead. But Wilde had always had suicidal tendencies. Why else would he ever have found his way into this business.

Numbers, letters, flickered through his brain. The correct sequence. It was a large Rover, painted black. It moved with infinite slowness, next to the pavement, chauffeur driven, the rear curtained and dark. A company director, heading for the luxury suburbs of Surrey, shutting the commonplace from his gaze. The car never altered speed. Wilde twisted the door handle, stepped inside, sat down. One moment he had been on the pavement, the next he was gone.

A light burned in the car's interior, hidden by the curtains from the crowds outside. Wilde discovered himself sitting next to a very young woman, on the far side of whom was a man reading *The Times,* which was now allowed to droop on to his lap. 'Good evening,' the man said. 'I think that went off very well. We shall certainly use this system again.'

His voice was quiet, accentless; each word was carefully pronounced. His mouth was small, but then, none of his features was large, and every one joined every other to make an almost flawless picture, not especially handsome, very far from ugly. His eyes were opaque, sleepy, hazel in colour. His black hair was flecked with grey, and was brushed straight back from his forehead, with no parting. His was a face one saw a hundred times in every day, in every office, in the back seat of every expensive car, in every good restaurant. It had no single aspect on which the mind could seize, and hold, and retain for future reference. He wore a blue business suit under a Burberry topcoat. His bowler hat hung from a hook next to his head, and beneath it waited his umbrella. His black shoes were highly polished. He gazed at Wilde without revealing either pleasure or distaste, even interest.

'*You* were late,' Wilde pointed out. 'And the temperature is just about zero.' He took off his gloves, slapped his hands together, smiled at the young woman. 'But it's warmer in here.'

'My dear fellow,' Sir Gerald said. 'I had every intention of being late. Had I been early, and had you not yet arrived, can you imagine the time it would have taken me to have regained that position, in this bedlam? Her name is Melanie.'

She was remarkably young. Far too young to be the personal secretary of a man like Sir Gerald Light, surely. And like her employer, she gave the impression of being totally featureless. Her hair was a light brown, and had a slight curl, although she was endeavouring to wear it straight. It lay on her shoulders. Her features were of the gamin variety, and she had brown eyes. The eyes promised more than the rest of her; they were lively, and looked at Wilde with a knowledgeable interest, although her smile was mechanical. It was difficult to decide about the rest of her; she wore a brown maxicoat, and brown boots. But the shoulders were narrow, even in the coat, and Wilde did not suppose there would be too much to hold on to underneath. Anyone less like Felicity Hart could hardly be imagined.

'Makes a change,' he remarked, and realised he was speaking, and thinking, the absolute truth. Sign of the times. For five years, while he had used his wife to answer the telephone, to be nothing more than a cog in the machine, to look at, from time to time, Sir Gerald Light had needed a beautiful and sexually provocative secretary. Now he made do with an extract from the typists' pool. But she was still too young.

He'd forgotten that Sir Gerald was a mind reader. Wilde's mind at any rate. 'Melanie has been training for five years,' Sir Gerald said. 'And she is only nineteen. I obtained her from an orphanage.'

He might have been speaking of an antique commode. She continued to gaze at Wilde.

'She had all the necessary qualifications, even at fourteen.' Sir Gerald was clearly pleased with his selection. 'High I.Q., loyalty, quiet tastes, ability and desire to work hard, unconventional outlook . . . would you say that summed you up, Melanie?'

The girl nodded.

'To which splendid armoury of talents,' Sir Gerald continued, 'she adds another most desirable feature, in any woman, but most especially in any employee of mine.'

It occurred to Wilde that after so many years of close contact he should no longer be surprised by anything this peculiar man said, or wished, or commanded to be done. But the utter contempt with which Sir Gerald regarded life itself, and the little fears and taboos and conventions which go to make up civilisation, always surprised him. He suspected it frightened him, too.

'An accident in her childhood,' Sir Gerald explained.

'Presumably she *can* communicate,' Wilde remarked.

Melanie's hands moved with the speed of some Western hero producing his Colt, and filled with a notebook, already opened, and a pencil, already moving at great speed. Wilde leaned over, and read, 'I love you, too.'

'You and I have just got to have a chat, sweetheart.' He folded his arms, squeezed each tricep; they were sore from the blows they had received in the alleyway.

'I'm sure you will get on,' Sir Gerald decided. 'You see, Wilde, I never had any doubts that Felicity would eventually have to be replaced. She was a most remarkable woman, in every way, but she came to me already a woman. Women, for all the nonsense poured out by certain obviously ill-informed novelists, are far less flexible than men. They give the impression of *being* flexible, of adjusting to circumstances, to their husbands, to their jobs, to the various misfortunes of life. But underneath it all, they remain themselves, true to whatever convictions, whatever certainties, they may have

accumulated in their formative years. Not even our Communist
friends have ever had any real success in brainwashing women
agents, which is why we use so many of them. So do our friends
in Washington. So do the Russians, for that matter. Our
Oriental acquaintances even prefer to use them in open diplo-
macy. Of course, horses for courses, as you know. A woman's
pain threshold is as a rule much lower than a man's. She will
break under physical mistreatment, and confess, where a man
might hold out until death. On the other hand, once she is released from pain, or from anything else, she reverts immediately to being herself, where a man can remain seduced from
reality for a very long time. In some cases, forever, as we know
to our cost. So, it is possible to lay down a rule, for people in
our position: Use men for couriers, women for permanence or
straightforward negotiation.'

Wilde sighed. 'It's a theory.' The sixth former and the
headmaster. It was an inescapable feeling, in this man's
company. But now it was the sixth former and the headmaster's wife. It was even possible that Sir Gerald was not
talking at large, as he appeared, but being very specific indeed. But if he was, he had to be raking up the past. Even
Sir Gerald, having been out all day, could not yet have
listened to a tape recording of his wife's telephone call.

'So Felicity, having certain ideas of her own about life,
remained always true to those ideas, however much I, and
you, Wilde, may have tried to alter her point of view. As I
knew she would. Thus I decided, quite some time ago, to
take a leaf from Moscow's book. Catch them young. Train
them and educate them and plant all the ideas yourself.
And make them loyal, by giving them what they really want
in life. And by making them feel wanted. Have I left anything out, Melanie?'

Melaine shook her head. She continued to gaze at Wilde,
smiling.

'Ah,' Sir Gerald said. 'She likes you, Wilde. Strange, how
women always do. You seem to possess some kind of animal

magnetism. But I must warn you not to get too close, Melanie. You haven't been formally introduced, have you? His name is Jonas Wilde. Code Name Eliminator. He is, I'm afraid, a professional murderer.'

3

MELANIE continued to smile at Wilde.

'And still she is fascinated,' Sir Gerald said. 'Of course, my dear girl, Wilde does not think of himself as a murderer. Neither do I. He would prefer the title of Executioner in Chief for H.M. Government. So would I. But facts are facts. Are they not, my dear boy? Ah, we seem to have arrived.'

The car had stopped. Wilde opened his door, got out, held it for Melanie. 'I can be quite friendly,' he said. 'Just so long as I have my two plates of raw meat, every day.' He looked around him. They were in a courtyard, somewhere back in Mayfair, he estimated. He had described a circle. 'Where from here?'

'Through that door,' Sir Gerald said. 'We have been invited to a party.'

Wilde followed them into a lobby, rather bleak, but recently and expensively decorated. The porter was a large man with a naturally grim face.

'Mr. Morrissey?' Sir Gerald asked. 'Are we at the right place?'

The porter picked up his telephone dialled a number. His gaze seemed able to envelop the three of them at once.

'My, ah, name, is Light,' Sir Gerald said.

'Sir Gerald Light, and party,' the porter said. He had a Midwest accent. He nodded, replaced the telephone. 'Go right up.'

Wilde followed Melanie and Sir Gerald into the lift. He

could only wait. But he was used to waiting. He had survived more than a dozen years in his peculiar profession, thanks to the cultivation of two strengths. One of them was patience.

But he could not resist the temptation to even the score, just a little. 'And how is Lady Light?' he asked, politely.

Sir Gerald never turned his head. 'She is very well, thank you, Wilde. I will tell her you inquired.'

Melanie gazed from one to the other, no longer smiling. She was intelligent. She had seen, or felt, the exchange. He wondered if she'd been allowed to meet Catherine.

The lift stopped, the doors opened. Melanie led them across a lobby carpeted in mauve, pressed a bell. This door also opened, immediately, allowed the escape of a blast of pop music, an aroma of alcohol, a cloud of cigarette smoke, and a cacophony of laughter and raised voices. In the midst of it all there was an extremely pretty dark-haired girl, wearing an orange catsuit. 'Hi,' she said. 'So glad you could make it. Come on in.' Florida, Wilde decided.

Behind her was a large sitting room, presently crowded. There were all ages, about equally divided as to sexes. Some stood at the bar, others danced to a radiogram, others smooched in corners. The girl waved her arm. 'I'm Betty,' she said. 'I won't bother introducing you. I figure you know everybody. Hi, Coolidge. Why don't you get these people a drink.'

The man was enormous, as tall as Wilde and twice as heavy. His face was as hard as a blacksmith's anvil; his nose and chin thrust forward like prongs. Even when he smiled, only his eyes showed pleasure. 'How's the Med?' he asked. He ignored Sir Gerald and Melanie.

Wilde had his fingers crushed. 'Warmer than here.'

'Not *here*,' the American said. 'Not *here*. This is where it's at.' He escorted them through the throng. No one took any notice. At the far end of the room there was a low coffee table, surrounded by a settee and three chairs. A man rose from the settee. He wore glasses, and was below medium

height; strain lines raced away from the corners of his eyes
and depressed his mouth. But Wilde was interested only in
what was *in* his eyes, and in his hands. He had thin fingers,
and they were dry. His eyes had the opacity that frightens.
It was going to be a business conference.

'Hi, Gerald,' he said. 'Good to see you.' He gazed at
Melanie and Wilde.

'Melanie Bird is my secretary,' Sir Gerald said. 'And this
is Wilde. Mr. Martin Clamp.'

'And I'm Coolidge Lucinda,' the big man said, shaking
Melanie's hand.

'Mr. Lucinda runs an organisation similar to ours in the
United States, Melanie,' Sir Gerald said. 'Although, of
course, as they go in for a somewhat greater division of
labour over there than we do over here, he has less outside
responsibilities, and therefore less distractions.'

Melanie smiled at each of the men in turn.

'And what does Mr. Clamp run?' Wilde asked.

'Sit down,' Clamp said, and did so. 'Coolidge, what about
some drinks.'

The girl Betty was hovering. 'Sherry for Sir Gerald,
Betty,' Lucinda said. 'Bristol Milk. Wilde will have a cocktail.'

'Martinis or daiquiris?' she asked.

'Rum, every time.'

'I told you so,' Lucinda said. 'And how about you, Miss
Melody Bird?'

'I'm sure a daiquiri will suit Melanie very well.' Sir Gerald
sat in one of the chairs. Lucinda took the other. Wilde sat
next to Clamp, and Melanie sat on his right. At least from
here he could watch the dancing; some of it was way out.

'All C.I.A.?' he asked.

'Just enough to keep an eye on things,' Lucinda said.
'The rest are Embassy staffers. Except Betty. She's my
London secretary.'

'Best secretary possible,' Clamp said. 'Let's get the business over with so we can go grab something. You're Jonas Wilde, eh? Coolidge has been telling me about you. Says you're old buddies.'

His voice was just audible above the steady beat of the music, and between him and the door there were at least twenty highly trained young men and women, every one eager to protect their boss. Wilde wondered if it made Sir Gerald jealous. 'We started off trying to kill each other,' he agreed. 'Then realised we were both wasting our time.'

'Yeah,' Clamp said. 'From what he says, he may have been the lucky one. Is it true you never use a gun?'

'Quite false,' Wilde said. 'I have often used a pistol, in self-defence.'

'But he prefers to leave them alone, in the line of duty,' Sir Gerald said. 'They are noisy, and smelly, and bloody, and carry things like fingerprints. Jonas has unearthed a unique method of execution, Martin. A swinging blow delivered at the base of the skull, in an *upwards* direction, with the flat of the hand. The word upwards is the operative one. The unique aspect, which make it different to any similar blow, far more lethal than a karate chop. Death is caused by the impact fracturing the odontoid process, which is a wad of tissue situated at the rear of the skull, protecting the medulla, which, as you will know, Martin, is that portion of the brain which operates the automatic functions of the body, breathing, heartbeat, and so on. The odontoid process is driven into the medulla, and that is that. Immediate, silent, no blood or other mess involved, and with the added virtue that death takes place in an exactly similar manner to that caused by a judicial hanging, which, of course, was a method long practised in this country.'

Clamp gazed at Wilde. 'But you don't use it any more.'

'Not for criminals, *per se*,' Sir Gerald said. 'We regard them as more sinned against by society, than, ah, sinning.

But Wilde does not oppose himself to criminals. He is a
weapon of the state. So are the U.S. Marines, and the
hydrogen bomb. Wilde is less expensive to maintain. On the
whole.'

'And it's *British*,' Wilde murmured, and smiled at an
over-developed blonde doing a shake by herself on the far
side of the room. She smiled back.

Melanie was scribbling on her pad. She passed it to Sir
Gerald.

'Oh, indeed, my dear,' he agreed. 'The force required to
deal such a blow effectively is enormous. But Wilde seems
able to exert it. He practises, you know.'

'Not on human beings,' Wilde said.

'Yeah,' Clamp said. 'Yeah . . . well . . .' He glanced at a
smiling Lucinda. 'I'm not sure just how these people like to
do business.'

Lucinda waited while Betty placed a tray on the coffee
table, and rejoined the party. 'They like it straight, Marty.
We want to borrow your boy, Sir Gerald.'

(ii)

'Hire,' Clamp said.

'How very remarkable,' Sir Gerald said. 'With this very
large and efficient organisation of yours, Mr. Lucinda, you
need to requisition my only operative? In this particular
field, at any rate. I take it we are discussing Wilde's own
particular field?'

'Yeah,' Lucinda said.

'The fact is,' Clamp said. 'It's to do with the Walner
business. We have a lead.'

'I find that hard to believe as well,' Sir Gerald said.

'Yeah. Well, let's say it *could* be a lead. A tip, actually.
What you fellows call a grass.'

'I would call it information received,' Sir Gerald said.
'From a reliable source?'

'No,' Lucinda said. 'We know nothing about the source

whatsoever. But we can't afford to hang around, Sir G. I
think your police force is the best in the world, and I regard
myself as a policeman. So they haven't got anywhere, yet. It
could happen, any minute. In fact, it *will* happen. So maybe
we're clutching at straws. I think we should at least take a
close look at this tip, and Marty agrees with me. We want
Jonas to take the look, and act upon it, if he can. That
figures, on two counts. First because he has no links with us,
and second because he's the best in the business.'

Sir Gerald sipped his sherry. 'I think I'd like a cigar,' he
said. 'Do you have such a thing?'

'I imagine Betty will be able to find you one,' Lucinda
said.

'He can have one of mine.' Wilde opened his pocket case.
'The name is Belfleur. Jamaican, not Havana. But every bit
as good.'

Sir Gerald held it to his nose, produced a silver cutter
and snipped the end. 'I will try anything, once.'

Wilde handed him a box of matches. 'Now, I hate to
spoil what's obviously going to be a super evening, Coolidge,
but like the man says, I work for H.M.G. It's not patriotism,
the money isn't all that good, and I don't expect that when
I get into trouble it will do me any good at all, but it helps
the conscience.'

'He thinks of himself as a private soldier.' Sir Gerald
remarked. 'Carrying out orders. My orders. But I am here,
Wilde. So far as you are concerned, I *am* H.M.G. So if I
agree to your, ah, secondment, the responsibility will surely
be mine. Now do be quiet, and listen, very carefully. I am
inclined to agree with Mr. Lucinda, and Mr. Clamp, that
we are faced with a serious situation. When I said just now,
that you did not oppose criminals, I meant ordinary criminals, of course. You police the, ah, underworld of interna-
tional relations, just as does Mr. Lucinda and his various,
ah, henchmen, and indeed, your own colleagues in my
employ. You are required to, ah, eliminate only those
traitors whose continued existence would be dangerous to

the future of this country of the Western Alliance, or known
enemy agents who are similarly regarded.'

Wilde sighed, and lit a cigar for himself. Sir Gerald, he
suspected, had always secretly yearned to be a politician.
And the blonde had found a partner.

'What would you say, if I asked you to eliminate a foreign
scientist, or a foreign politician, merely because he happened
to be working in a direction which *could* be against our
national interests?'

'This girl of yours makes a damned good daiquiri,
Coolidge,' Wilde said.

Lucinda signalled Betty.

'Quite so,' Sir Gerald said. 'I should consider such a state
of affairs as being in extremely poor taste. After all, how
could we carry on a civilised existence in those circumstances?
I'm afraid I regard political assassination as the very lowest
form of crime.'

Betty presented her tray.

'Would you care to join us?' Wilde asked. 'We're over-
weighted with men, this end of the room.'

She smiled at him. 'You join me, later.'

'You may find it amusing, Wilde,' Sir Gerald said. 'But
I'm afraid a series of assassinations has taken place in this
country during the past two years which has been causing
the police, and the government, and, naturally, myself, a
great deal of concern. I am not going to bore you with the
details, but in the past twenty-four months seven important,
ah, people, have been murdered. Their names are not relevant, but you may take it as read that the deaths are all
connected, and point to the same person.'

'I don't remember reading about any sensational murder
cases in the Marseilles newspapers,' Wilde said.

'Fortunately, up to now, we have succeeded in hushing
the deaths up, as murders. They were put down to heart
attacks. You may recall that a similar series of events took
place in the Soviet Union a few years ago, the victims at

that time being generals. It remains impossible to apportion any guilt for those, even at a national level, and however great may be one's suspicions. And so, unfortunately, has been the case with our own misfortunes. But these men were murdered. Make no mistake about that.'

'I don't see where there is an American involvement,' Wilde said.

'Maybe I should take over about here, Sir Gerald,' Lucinda said. 'We're involved, Jonas, because the seven dead men are all Americans.'

(iii)

Wilde sipped his daiquiri. The blonde girl had disappeared altogether.

'But all in England,' he said.

'Yes, indeed,' Sir Gerald said. 'Which puts H.M.G. in rather a, ah, hot seat.'

'It's goddamned serious,' Lucinda said. 'As you know, Jonas, no matter what the newspapers, and the odd politicians, spout, we work pretty close. The old war-time liaison was never really broken down, in military and scientific fields. It never will be, so long as the present government obtains in Moscow. And in Peking. So there are quite a few of your top people working under cover in the States, and vice versa. Or there were. Now there are seven less, of ours. Like Sir Gerald says, they all died of heart attacks. Up to now. But even up to now, the word has been getting around. You know how it is. What happened to old Jones? Oh, he died. In the U.K. Nothing odd about that. And old Smith? Oh, he died too. In the U.K. Say, old Brown, where are you going next? The U.K. Gulp. So maybe old Brown asks to duck this one. That's how it's *been*. But last week there was the seventh death. And this one is going to explode right in our faces. Marty?'

Martin Clamp got out of his chair with a sigh, knelt and

then sat on the floor, and then lay down on his back, with
his knees up. None of the dancers paid him any attention.

'Do you have back trouble?' Wilde asked. 'I suffered
from it once. It's a nervous complaint, you know.'

'So I'm nervous,' Clamp said. 'Kevin Walner. Originally
a Hungarian, defected at the time of the '56 uprising,
naturalised American. Top-ranking chemist. Last year he
was sent over here to take charge of a defence laboratory in
which we happen to have a shade more know-how than you
people. Just what they're making is not relevant. The important point with Walner is that his work was of a highly
secret and dangerous nature, and second, and more important, that it *was* secret. Even the fact that he worked for the
State Department is, and always was, a secret. He was
covered as an analgesic expert, on loan to the British sub-
sidiary of one of our American drug companies. He was
listed as a director, even bought a house in your stockbroker
belt, kept regular office hours, commuted like everyone else.
Last week he died.'

Wilde finished his drink. 'And Walner's death bothers
you where the previous six didn't.'

'We have been going wild,' Clamp said. 'I beg your pardon. Crazy. Over this thing. So have your police. But it was
at least a theory that someone was trying to convince
Americans that working in the U.K. wasn't good for the
healths. Those first six victims were known to be connected
with the State Department. Walner had no known connection with us whatsoever.'

'So they, the murderer and his employers, *may* just be
casting a wider net,' Lucinda said. 'Or they *may* just know
who Walner really was, and what he was working on.'

Sir Gerald relit his cigar. 'Which would be unfortunate.
For all of us.'

'Yeah,' Clamp said. 'That's one way of putting it.'

'There's no other possible connection between the seven
deaths?' Wilde asked. 'Something to do with Hungary,
maybe?'

'Not a chance,' Lucinda said. 'None of the first six had ever been to Hungary in their lives.'

'Adamson had never even been to Europe,' Clamp said sadly.

'You mentioned a grass,' Wilde said. 'To the murderer, or to his employer?'

'Oh, to the murderer, Mr. Wilde,' Clamp said. 'We think the information is a private matter, and that we are dealing with someone who perhaps is in your profession, but on a more mercenary basis, and there has been a disagreement close to home. Don't worry, finding the employer is Coolidge's problem, and he has some ideas. Trouble is, now there's been a tip, we have to act, fast. As we said, Walner's death wasn't like the other six. They *did* appear like natural deaths, and so the police and the government have been able to keep it cool, officially. But there's going to be no hushing up the Walner business. It's already been headline news, and unfortunately, that tip was not given to me as an individual, but to the Embassy. Now, the Ambassador believes in doing things right, and that information is going to be passed along to Scotland Yard tomorrow morning. I managed to stall it this long, until I could talk with you and Sir Gerald, but that's as far as I can go. And we can't afford to have our man arrested for murder. If he does happen to know what Walner was working on, he might just blow the lot.'

'You have got to reach him before the police do, Jonas,' Lucinda said.

'Rather summary justice, wouldn't you say, Coolidge?' Wilde asked. 'Is it *that* important?'

'Yes,' said Sir Gerald.

'So may I ask a question? Or two?'

'Shoot,' Lucinda invited.

'There's no doubt at all that Walner was killed by the same man who did the other six?'

'None at all,' Lucinda said.

'But you suggested there was a difference in method.'

'No,' Lucinda said. 'Only in approach. The first six were

all found dead in their cars, in the evening, somewhere in London. They were all unhurt. They had all, apparently, been drinking, and appeared, as Sir Gerald says, to have had heart attacks. Up to post-mortem time. But in the case of Walner, two people showed up at his *house,* at five o'clock in the afternoon. It was last week, so it was already dark. But still, a hell of an early hour to start that kind of thing. They knocked on the door, and when one of the children opened it, they came in. They tied up the two children and Mrs. Walner, and just waited for Walner to come home. Seems they were very pleasant, switched on the TV, poured themselves a cup of tea—gloves—kept the conversation going. But Mom and the kids were tied up and gagged. Then Walner came home, and was removed, at gunpoint. Mrs. Walner thought, and she thinks her husband did too, that he was being kidnapped, by people who wanted to find out something about his job. Both the murderers kept assuring them that no one was going to get hurt.'

'I can't say I like the way these people are multiplying,' Wilde said. 'I had the impression it was *a* murderer you were after.'

'Basically,' Lucinda said. 'Now, the murder took place about fifteen minutes after leaving the house, according to the coroner. Walner was taken away in his own car. Maybe he even drove it, but I wouldn't like to swear to that. In any event, fifteen minutes after leaving his house he was given what a doctor would call a terminal injection; air. He would have died within seconds. There is no evidence of any struggle, or even any restraint, so he would appear to have accepted the injection voluntarily.'

'There was the brandy,' Clamp said.

'Oh, sure,' Lucinda agreed. 'He apparently took a slug of brandy just prior to his death, but hardly sufficient to render him incapable. Anyway, as I said, death took place within seconds. The car was then driven into London, parked down some quiet sidestreet, Walner was left behind the wheel, and the killers walked away. When he was discovered, it appeared that he had had a heart attack.'

'What about the transport used by the murderers to reach Walner's home?' Wilde asked.

'Abandoned right outside his house. It was stolen, of course.'

'And the police haven't been able to find a thing? What about descriptions? Going on your sad tale, Coolidge, Mrs. Walner and her two kids must have had a pretty good look at these people.'

'They wore masks in the house,' Lucinda said. 'And you know how it is, description wise.' He took a notebook from his pocket, flipped it open. 'A man and a girl, to be precise. We suspect her business was driving and just generally helping out. The man did most of the talking.'

'There must be *some* description going,' Wilde said.

'Oh, sure. The woman was short and thin. Probably fair, but she wore a headscarf as well as a mask. The man was described as tall, well built, soft-spoken.'

'English?'

'Spoken without accent. You'll agree there isn't much to go on. Now, the body was found by a beat policeman at eight o'clock that night. As I said, first estimates were that he'd been drinking, the smell of brandy, you see, and then had had a heart attack. The murderer had promised Mrs. Walner that he'd telephone the police and have them released in an hour, but he never did, and the poor woman, and her kids, were still sitting there at eight-thirty, when the hospital telephoned. They couldn't get a reply, so they called the local police instead. Even the hospital, at that time, assumed it was a heart attack. It wasn't until Mrs. Walner started spouting that things started to happen, and even then it took time. It was ten o'clock before any sort of general alarm went out.'

'And produced nothing,' Wilde said.

'Not a sausage. Repeating each earlier pattern. You can use the cliché about thin air. But that's the thing about professional, apparently motiveless murderers. As you know, Jonas.'

'Oh, indeed,' Wilde agreed. 'So there the matter rested until your tip. Which was?'

Clamp reached into his inside breast pocket, produced a sheet of paper, handed it to Wilde. The words were printed: WALNER'S KILLER IS NAMED O'DOWD. YOU'LL FIND HIM AT DORT.

(iv)

'Which is a village in the Medoc,' Lucinda said.

Wilde handed the sheet to Sir Gerald. 'The Word means sleep.'

'So maybe it's a sleepy little village,' Lucinda agreed. 'I looked it up. It's actually on the left bank of the Gironde, say twenty-odd miles downriver from Bordeaux. Know the area, Jonas?'

'I took my boat down to the Med through the Midi Canal, if that's what you mean. So I must have motored past Dort, according to you. Can't say I remember it.'

'At least you'll be sure the wine will be drinkable,' Lucinda said.

'You intend to act on this?'

Lucinda glanced at Clamp.

The Embassy official slowly sat up. 'Well, as Mr. Lucinda said just now, Mr. Wilde, this is an urgent matter. Not only because tomorrow that note goes to Scotland Yard, but because we can't tell how these people are going to play it next. Maybe Walner *was* just an extension of their net. But it's more likely they *do* know something about his work. And there's another possibility: if these people are out to sabotage the confidential links between Washington and London they may be getting fed up at the way we've managed to hush the whole business up, so far. The first six victims were lifted in town, just after they left their offices, real quiet like. Walner was taken with a band playing, just about. So the line stops here. Now, according to what Mr. Lucinda has told me about you and your methods, this should be just a piece of cake, for you. You have a French village, and a man named O'Dowd. There can't be any difficulty about that. Just go there, pick your time and place —naturally we want it done right away—and ease back out. Mr. Lucinda will look after your exit.'

'Sammy Bennett's on the job. You remember Sammy, Jonas?'

'How could I ever forget him.' Wilde rubbed his chin. 'Well, like I said, Dort is on the banks of the river, and I understand it has some kind of a dock. Sammy's on his way there now, with a boat of ours. He'll pick you up. Today is Tuesday. Tomorrow morning Sammy will be in Royon. That's the little port at the mouth of the river.'

'I've been there,' Wilde said.

'On the rising tide, tomorrow evening, Sammy will go upriver to Bordeaux, and spend the night there. He'll start coming downriver Thursday evening, against the tide. It turns to the ebb at oh four hundred on Friday morning. Sammy will come alongside at Dort at oh three fifty-five. You'll step aboard, and you'll carry the tide the rest of the way. By dawn you'll be out of the river and into the bay. There'll be nothing to connect the stranger who was hanging around Dort with Sammy's boat, and it's got a special cubbyhole for you to dive into just in case you *are* hailed by the coast-guard. We've used it before, or at least a similar model, off Cuba. Believe me, it works.' He grinned. 'It'll be like old times, using a boat to exit.'

'Oh, I believe you, Coolidge. I have the highest respect for Sammy's ability, even if I'm tickled pink at the idea of his working his way across the Bay of Biscay by boat, in December; he'll have a chilblain or two to remember. And as you say, it'll be like old times, except that I've never actually been at sea on Christmas Day, which is Sunday, as

I imagine you've forgotten. There's just one small thing. So far as I can see, not one of you has provided me with the slightest bit of proof that this chap O'Dowd, if he exists, and if he lives in Dort, if *it* exists, is guilty, or even connected, with these crimes. Just for instance, O'Dowd is an Irish name, wouldn't you say? Does Mrs. Walner recall the man speaking with an Irish accent?'

'Well, no,' Clamp said. 'But it is possible to lose an accent. Even an Irish accent.'

'As for your other point, Jonas,' Lucinda said. 'Dort does exist, and so does O'Dowd. I got hold of a telephone directory for the area, before I wasted my time asking for you. Charles O'Dowd, Dort. Apparently the place is so small the address doesn't need any qualification. The number is Dort 2. Only O'Dowd and the pension have telephones.'

'Which means he's somebody in the district.'

'The local British resident, perhaps,' Sir Gerald said. 'Or Irish resident, as the case may be. In any event, Wilde, I don't see that his guilt or innocence concerns you. I'm afraid in recent years you have been showing a tendency to become more and more *involved* in our work. It's a mistake, psychologically.'

'You wouldn't say that when I'm sent out to kill a man, I'm involved with him?' Wilde asked pleasantly.

'The word is eliminate, remember? You're no more involved than a front-line soldier is involved with the enemy against whom he discharges his rifle, as you yourself once understood. The decision is ours, Mr. Clamp's and my own. We have assessed the situation, and decided that O'Dowd is our man. That is all that need concern you.'

Melanie Bird picked up her empty glass, looked into it.

'That was a mighty rapid assessment,' Wilde said. 'Seeing that you didn't know O'Dowd existed until you came in.'

'Those daiquiries really travel,' Lucinda said. 'The john is through here, Jonas.'

The dancers were looking pretty weary, by now; perhaps they hadn't expected their boss's conference to last this long. Wilde followed Lucinda into a bedroom, off which a door opened into a bathroom. The bed was presently occupied, by the blonde and a male friend. Lucinda smacked her bottom, which was available. 'Out,' he said. 'Tell Betty I want her. These kids are the goods,' he said. 'They never act. Tell them to have a ball, and they do just that.'

'It's the only way.' It was a woman's room, brushes, perfumes, cosmetics, lace curtains.

Lucinda was in the bathroom. 'So it's nasty. You ever enjoyed *any* aspect in our business?'

'Once,' Wilde said. 'When I was very, very young. The new boy.' He lay across the bed. Suddenly he was very tired. 'Remember? I used to look at myself as the knight in shining armour, combating the ungodly, whom the ordinary processes of the law couldn't touch.'

'Comic book stuff,' Lucinda said. 'Believe me, Jonas, I'm unhappy about having to point the finger at O'Dowd. Maybe he won't be there. Maybe it's a bum steer.'

'In which case?'

Lucinda leaned against the bureau. 'Have yourself a couple of cases of Latour, on me. They tell me the '46 is pretty good, right now.'

'It's the '44,' Wilde said. 'And it'll cost you a packet. I'd rather have a case of Château Dort. It's a good wine, you know, only third growth, but distinctive. And it's been scarce, the last year or so.'

'So you're a wine snob. When you've finished, catch Sammy and come home.'

The door opened and Betty came in. She smiled at Wilde, went into the bathroom, closed the door.

'She has good taste in beds,' Wilde said. 'But you think O'Dowd will be there.'

'I *know* there is an O'Dowd in Dort, and I *think* the tip is genuine, yes. Hell, Jonas, this isn't a burglary, or even a gang killing, with someone out to do the dirty on an old boy friend. Kevin Walner was kidnapped and murdered. Your newspapers have given it full publicity, but not a hint that

the State Department was involved. Yet that note was sent
to the Embassy.'

'And Walner's business was *that* secret?'

'I'm afraid it was. Look, Jonas, I have no desire to gun
down an innocent man. You can catch a flight to Bordeaux
tomorrow morning, which will give you all of twenty-four
hours. It'd be simple enough to find out a thing or two,
mainly if this chap O'Dowd was there on Wednesday of
last week, or not.'

'Circumstantial evidence.'

Betty came out of the bathroom, sat in a chair. She sat
very straight, knees together, hands relaxed on her lap.

'Added to the note,' Lucinda said. 'That's proof. I can't
offer you more than that.'

'What about the woman?'

'Only if you have to, Jonas. Mrs. Walner got the impression the woman was nervous. The man wasn't. So she's a
sidekick. O'Dowd is the one we want.'

'I'm counting my blessings.' Wilde stubbed out his cigar.
'And you won't use one of yours. Don't get me wrong,
Coolidge. I gave up expecting the truth years ago. I don't
even *want* it, nowadays. But this tale of yours has so many
holes, it isn't even amusing.'

Lucinda sighed. 'Sometimes I wish you *were* just a walking muscle. Okay, Jonas. We know who's behind this. But
we can't do anything about them, right this minute. That's
White House talk. Now we've a lead on their hatchet man,
we *can* do something about him. But not my boys. If anything were to go wrong, and an American to be arrested for
the murder of Charles O'Dowd, we may as well start swop-
ping missiles.'

'Whereas a wandering Englishman would be just quietly
guillotined. Sooner or later. My boat is still in Sete.'

'You won't be a wandering Englishman, Jonas. You'll be
Jules Romain, from Belgium, in France on business. You
speak French, I'm told.'

'Fluently. But not with a Flemish accent.' Wilde sat up.

'And should anything go wrong, Sammy won't go within
ten miles of Dort?'

'Should anything go wrong, Jules Romain won't be on the
dock. There's nothing to connect Sammy with anything
which may have happened ashore while he's cruising up and
down the river. The important thing is, Jonas, that with
you around, things don't *go* wrong. And afterwards, why
should anyone connect Jules Romain, itinerant Belgian murderer of Bordeaux, with Jonas Wilde, itinerant English
yachtsman of Sete? So the two places are maybe a shade too
close for comfort. You weren't planning on spending the
rest of your life there, were you? Come to think of it, if
you've been there since September, you'd better get
a move on, or you'll be having trouble with French
customs.'

'I was planning on Malta, in a week or so,' Wilde agreed.
'Did you say Romain?'

Betty sat beside Wilde on the bed. 'One passport,
Belgian. Coolidge tells me you have some spare photo-
graphs. One driving licence, Belgian. Two credit cards. A
letter from a friend. Female.'

'You've an efficient girl here, Coolidge.'

'It'd pay you to be, too, Jonas. So to Marty and Gerald
this is a piece of cake, to someone with your experience. But
you don't want to forget that O'Dowd is a professional, too.
For instance, he knew the names of the Walner children, he
knew which afternoon was the maid's day off, he and his
girl friend seemed very much at home with their weapons,
small automatic pistols, and the man, at least, struck Jane
Walner as being very cool and competent. So I still don't
think he's in your class, and you'll have the advantage of
surprise. But O'Dowd's no pussycoat.'

'Yeah,' Wilde said. 'So I'll go back and smile at the two
buzzards, shall I?'

'In a moment. Betty has something else for you.'

'Fifteen thousand dollars, in U.S. currency,' she said,
placing the bundle beside the passport.

'We thought we'd offer a bit more than your normal fee,' Lucinda said. 'As it's a one off.'

'Charity week,' Wilde murmured, pocketing the money.

'Call it a pension, if you like. Just in case you felt like asking Sammy to drop you in Spain, instead of England.'

Wilde glanced at him. Lucinda moved his head, and Betty got up. 'Don't forget you asked me to dance,' she said to Wilde, and left the room.

'You shouldn't ever settle, even for three months, while you're still in the business,' Lucinda said. 'So you've been soaking up the sun in Sete just a shade too long. One of my boys spotted you, back in September.'

'Your boys have identification?'

'*My* boys, Jonas. Strictly mine. I wouldn't want another balls-up ever to happen again. Someone might just get killed.'

'I'll bear that in mind.'

'So Monkton went down that way at the beginning of December, and there you still were, growing weeds on the bottom of your boat. He filed a report with me, wanted to know if you were out to stud. Which is one reason why, when this came up, you were in my mind. One reason why I opted for you, so quick. But Monkton was still around. You know what, Jonas? Like I said, when you're on the job, you're still the best in the business. But when you're relaxing, nowadays, you're goddamned careless. You've stopped looking over your shoulder. And it occurs to me that there might be one or two other people in the world would recognise you on sight.'

'So your boy put glue on his hands,' Wilde said, very quietly. 'Maybe he even wound up in an ice bucket.'

'A newspaper in the lobby was sufficient.'

'So how did Monkton reach you? I only left the hotel an hour ago.'

'He called, lunchtime. He figured you were upstairs for a while.'

'And you told him, stay on the job.' Wilde took the wallet from his breast pocket. 'He'll need this, when he gets over his bellyache.'

Lucinda opened the wallet, slowly. 'For Christ's sake.'

'Everybody makes mistakes. Your boy needs a new pair of shoes. Oh, sure, I was goddamned relieved when I realised he was yours. What beats me, Coolidge, is that you still expect me to work for you?'

'It won't happen again, Jonas. But I'm happy it did, this time. So sock it to me if you really want to, but there are easier ways to die.'

'Monkton travels with DeBrett?'

'He didn't know her from Raquel,' Lucinda said. 'But he gave me a description. God knows, I'm not much good at the Dutch uncle bit; I even get on with my own kids. I've heard you described as the most dangerous man in the world. I think that's a pretty fair description, when the chips are down and you're face to face with a situation. But unlike too many killers, you haven't gotten callous, with the years, and the jobs. Every one seems to bother you more and more. You know what that means? You're spending more and more time thinking about the other guy's point of view. Like with O'Dowd. That's bad, in your business. Because one day it's going to check your swing. Now Gerald, I don't think he ever saw any point of view in his life, but his own. Don't get me wrong. I think he's the best man possible for *his* job, and I thank God every morning that his desk is in Whitehall and not in the Kremlin. But watching the two of you together is like watching a lion tied up with a mamba.'

'Yeah.' Wilde washed his hands. 'So what's in it for you, Coolidge?'

'I happen to like you, boy. I always was a dumb bunny.' Lucinda opened the bedroom door. 'But if the going gets rough, you could maybe think of that fifteen thousand as a down payment.

(v)

As if it mattered, now. Wilde leaned back in his seat, looked at his watch. The time was eight-seventeen, the day was Wednesday; in less than an hour he'd be in Bordeaux. He wondered what the temperature was like, down there.

And now Sir Gerald would have his tape recording. As if it mattered.

It was difficult to estimate his reaction, accurately. It was difficult to suppose that ice-cold brain could ever work in any other than a totally logical sequence. He had married Catherine, in line with that logic. He had needed more than a secretary, a Girl Friday. He had needed an extra pair of hands, and an extra brain, always there, always trustworthy, an extension of himself. So why not take a wife? And if taking a wife, why not pick the best looks, and the best background, available within the range of necessary talent? So why not suspect that, after a while, she might get just a little lonely. But having worked the sequence out logically that far, it was also logical to suppose, to be quite sure, that her breeding and loyalty would prevent her going any farther. Logical, if your name happened to be Sir Gerald Light.

But no one could have foreseen the tremendous foul-up last spring, which had left Sir Gerald temporarily out of action, left Catherine running the show for a breathless seventy-two hours, with only Wilde to turn to. That had defied logic. Only, given those peculiar circumstances, what had followed had been logical enough. And that Wilde would call again had been a logical enough supposition. Unless someone did something to end it.

'Coffee?' The stewardess smiled at him. 'Sugar?'

'Two lumps.' She was a pretty girl. But pretty girls were a commodity he could do without, right this minute. Maybe he'd only realised how little they meant, last night, when he had danced with Betty. They meant nothing at all, any more. He looked through the window at the solid cloud base beneath the jet. Presumably they were over the English Channel, by now. It was near freezing down there, according to the newspaper.

But there was another break in the logical sequence of events: That Sir Gerald might react like a man, instead of a computer. Only twice, in eight months. Once out of curiosity. But the second time . . . had he really been on the ball, Wilde realised, he's have been strictly a cad and found out just when that second time had been.

As if it mattered. Because *he* had never been logical. He didn't think he had ever understood life, which was probably why he was such an efficient assassin. He had only ever been aware that life, twentieth-century life, was a sequence of events, of happenings, into which he did not fit. As Catherine had said, he was a savage, a throwback to some primeval ancestor. He would have enjoyed the stone age, when life was entirely a business of essentials.

He had been happy in Korea. As a soldier, he had been a misfit; his record showed that. As a lethal machine he had been in a class of his own. His record also showed that. So what better profession for a rootless savage, whose every venture into civilisation had been disastrous, than to continue as a lethal machine, for all time? For eternity. There was the rub. When he had gone to work for the Section, he had left his problems behind him. Problems had suddenly become irrelevant. No one had ever survived more than two or three years in the Section. Not in the field. Then, forty, even thirty, had seemed an unimaginable age to attain.

Now they were both behind him, and in the interim he had lost his sense of perspective, the essential knowledge of the difference between life and death. Sir Gerald and Lucinda, the two men who probably knew him better than any other men in the world, criticised his involvement. They only wanted the machine, not the man. Well, Sir Gerald did. Lucinda's friendship was genuine enough; that had been proved more than once. But Lucinda was one of

that unique, and happy breed of men, able to divorce his
vocation from his life. Lucinda kept his friends, on the right
side. Although, come to think of it, Lucinda was also crack-
ing, in that he had befriended Wilde.

And Lucinda had given him an out. Not from friendship, only, this time. Lucinda would really like to have Wilde
on his payroll. Even a Wilde past his prime, given to too
much involvement. Because Wilde was still the best in the
business. Something to think about.

But not right this moment. The aircraft was on the
ground, taxiing towards the Terminal Building, and he had
not given a thought to the assignment. Wilde, the man who
always planned so meticulously, and so survived. But then,
as Marty Clamp had suggested, this was surely a piece of
cake. However dangerous Charles O'Dowd might be, when
on the job, he had created for himself this bolthole, and here
he would relax. Wilde himself knew only too well the feeling
of safety once a self-made security had been reached. So he
might, at first sight, be suspicious of all strangers, but
Wilde would soon put a stop to that, with that tremendous
charm which was another of his stocks in trade. Wilde had
two whole days to take a careful look around, find O'Dowd,
and get O'Dowd alone, just for five seconds, preferably on
Thursday evening. Because that was all he needed. However O'Dowd expected the end to come, and being in this
business he had to expect it to come sooner or later, he
would think in normal terms, of guns and knives, of war-
rants of arrest. He would scarcely suspect that they would
send a man whose only weapon was his hands, because he
would not know Wilde. He would not know that Wilde
existed. He could not know that. Which was the greatest
of all Wilde's strengths.

So on Thursday evening, all things being equal, a bur-
glar would break into the O'Dowd residence, and in the
course of the burglary he would break Charles O'Dowd's
neck. The simplest plans were always the best.

But first thing was to get to Dort and have a look around.

He went to the Hertz desk. 'I'd like a car,' he said in French.

'Of course,' the girl agreed.

'Something small. A Simca?'

'For how long would you like it, Mr. . . . ?' She glanced at the driving licence which was lying open on the counter. 'Mr. Romain?'

'Two or three days.'

'Of course.' She inserted a carbon between two forms, began to write.

The man standing behind Wilde said, also in French, 'Perhaps you could let me have my keys, mademoiselle.'

'Of course,' she agreed, without raising her head. 'It is good to see you home, Mr. O'Dowd.'

4

WILDE wrote 'Jules Romain' at the bottom of the form. Clamp had said this assignment would be a piece of cake. But never before had he had a target thrust down his throat.

He glanced sideways, watched the man walking to the exit, carrying an overnight bag. He was about six feet tall, on the thin side, even in a topcoat, had little chin but a wide, cheerful mouth, a small nose, and shallow green eyes. His hair was fair, which was unexpected; but when he'd visited the Walners he had worn a hat. And he was well known, not only in his own neighbourhood, but in Bordeaux. At the airport. Because he was a frequent traveller?

Charles O'Dowd. The man who tied up women and children, and took their husbands out for terminal injections. It was necessary to think this, to begin right away the build-up to the killing hate, the white-hot anger which would be needed to take him through the next few hours.

'Thank you, sir,' said the girl. 'You will pay a deposit? Or put it on your credit card?'

Wilde gave her some French currency, watched O'Dowd unlock a Mercedes, throw his overnight bag into the back seat, get behind the wheel.

'Thank you, sir,' said the girl. 'There will be a refund, of course. Now, here is the key. It is the first Simca in the rank. You may leave it at any of our offices.'

'Thanks.' Wilde picked up his overnight bag, went outside. Two men with overnight bags. Two men in the same profession. One returning, the other arriving.

The Mercedes reversed out of parking without hurry, turned, drove towards the road. Wilde started his engine. He had checked the map on the aircraft; it was more than twenty miles from Bordeaux to Dort, and the road turned in towards the river. Judging by the map, there did not seem to be many villages, other than the town of Pauillac. The very name made him thirsty.

But he had not come here to sample the wines. He drove out of the car park, turned on to the road. The Mercedes was about three hundred yards in front of him, a nice, big, beautiful, conspicuous car, even if O'Dowd should visit the city first. But Wilde's decision had to be made now. Now meant no preparation, no proper investigation, no proper planning. Now meant forgetting Sammy Bennett. But now also meant Charles O'Dowd, totally unsuspicious, totally unprotected, perhaps even more relaxed than he would be when he reached his destination, because now he was on the last lap to security.

And now also meant no link between Jules Romain and Charles O'Dowd. Jules Romain would not even have been to Dort. And afterwards? A hire car turned in at somewhere like La Rochelle, a man named Romain, should police investigations take them that far. A man with no motive or connection to the murder. What about his background? An airline seat, purchased in London. A car, hired in

Bordeaux for a drive north. If the girl at the airport remembered that Mr. Romain and Mr. O'Dowd had arrived together, she had still only looked at Wilde once. And by then Jules Romain would no longer exist. He would have caught a train at La Rochelle, and disappeared, perhaps heading north for his native Belgium. And a man called Wilde would have hired a car in St. Malo, announcing loudly that he was off the flight from Jersey, and driven across France to Sete, there to pick up his yacht.

And Sammy Bennett would take a trip up the Gironde, and go home again.

There would hardly be any better way to play it, provided he could find a suitably lonely stretch along the way. And provided he was prepared to accept Sir Gerald, and Clamp's decision. Which was his job. Lucinda had suggested he might check, dates and times, just to be sure. Sir Gerald would be horrified at the very idea.

They were skirting the city itself now, heading west. There was a great deal of traffic, mostly building up for the huge bridge which spans the river just below the yacht club. Wilde thought he might stop in Bordeaux for lunch, afterwards. That would be a sound idea, to establish that Jules Romain, at any rate, had not been in a hurry. Besides, he liked Bordeaux.

It was a good day, cold and crisp, with not a trace of ice and a lot of blue sky above. The traffic began to fade, and the Mercedes gathered speed. Suddenly they were in the country, represented by a fringe of trees to the right, endless fields of close-pruned, dwarf grape-vines to the left, and behind the fields, low hills, occasionally topped by a church or a château.

The Mercedes swung round a right-handed bend, and the trees parted for a moment, to allow a glimpse of the river, wide, swift moving, brown; they were just below the union of the Garonne and the Dordogne, with forty miles of the Gironde between them and the Bay of Biscay. And there was mist, creeping along the banks, resisting the efforts of the winter sun to dissipate it. Of course, there was early morning mist on the Gironde, every day, in the summer, usually it was dispersed by eleven, but apparently in the winter it lasted that much longer. The river disappeared moments after they saw it, as a white cloud drifted across, blanketing the road as well. For a few moments Wilde even lost the Mercedes, then it reappeared, much closer; O'Dowd had slowed.

He thought to himself, how goddamned ridiculous. Everything he could wish was happening before he wished it. In the mist there would be no risk of anyone seeing the Simca; seeing either car, for that matter. The mist was as good as the darkest night. And yet he was uneasy. The man, the moment, the place, all in his sights, all unasked. Not quite the moment, yet. Dort was several miles beyond Pauillac, and Pauillac could not be all that distant, now. Better to wait. There would be even less risk of other traffic, beyond Pauillac.

But the decision was taken, now. It had been taken the moment he had heard the girl call O'Dowd's name, at the airport. All that was needed was the killing hate, the power which would concentrate all of his weight into that swinging right hand, the power Sir Gerald liked to boast about, but would never understand. Because Sir Gerald did not hate. His view of the world was entirely pragmatic. Given certain considerations, which were to be regarded as important and unchanging—the country, the Western Alliance—everything else, anything which opposed or even touched these permanencies, had to be squashed, removed, destroyed. Eliminated. There was no need for passion in such a black and white world.

But passion did not only cover the emotion of hate. Passion meant a great many things. Passion covered love, and lust, emotions Sir Gerald had never felt. Except, perhaps, during this last summer. He had learned passion from Wilde, who lived on passion, because without it he was no more than an ordinary man. So now, perhaps, Sir Gerald could also hate. Who would be the first object of his hatred?

Houses rushed at them, and the Mercedes slowed some more. Pauillac, easily distinguishable because of its docks, the ever-glowing flame above the refinery. He had spent a night here on his way upriver in September, in the peculiar little yacht harbour formed by moored barges. Beyond Pauillac the road was empty, for some distance.

He shook his head. Personal thoughts, at a moment like this. *There* was madness. Certainly it would be dangerous to wait a moment longer than he had to, now. The refinery raced by on their left, and he allowed his foot to press the pedal; the Simca moved forward, closing the gap between the two cars. The mist was limiting visibility to about a quarter of a mile, and there were no houses visible within that range. That was not really good enough, not sure enough. It would not *be* good enough, in normal circumstances. Today it was ample. Because today Wilde was in a hurry. For one of the very rare times in his life his immense patience had deserted him. He wanted to be done with it, and leave, and think. He had too much to think about.

The Mercedes was immediately in front of him. He pulled out, into the middle of the road, drove his foot to the floor, and saw the lorry coming at him, looming out of the mist. To his left was an earth bank, promising only a cartwheel, in the very path of the lorry. Desperately he swung the wheel back to his right, gunning in the same instant. The circumstances for an entirely accidental car crash were suddenly as ready made as everything else in this crazy affair, even if the odds were that they would both be killed. But the driver of the Mercedes, recognising that the Simca was in trouble, had reacted instantly in the only possible way. He had also accelerated, and the additional horsepower of the big car had taken him screaming into the mist. Now there were only trees, and then water, to Wilde's right. Braking was useless. The swing had been too violent; there might not be any ice on the road, but there was certainly a lot of moisture. Wilde turned into the skid, and the Simca swung right round, before sliding sideways and into the ditch be-

side the road. There was a crunch of a crackling exhaust
muffler, of a folding rear wing, and then the car stopped,
and was silent, save for a low hum.

Wilde took out his handkerchief, and wiped his brow. So
much for that. Maybe next time he'd be able to keep his
mind on the job.

His door was pulled open, and the truck driver gazed at
him. 'But you are mad,' he said in French. 'In this visibility, mad.'

'I thought the road was clear.' Wilde also spoke in
French. He got out, watched the Mercedes reversing towards
him. He felt he was taking part in some surrealist play. A man
determined to stay close to death, at all costs.

O'Dowd got out. 'You are all right, monsieur?' he asked
in French.

'He is all right, Mr. O'Dowd,' said the truck driver. 'But
the car . . .'

O'Dowd frowned at Wilde. 'But you are the man from
the airport. The Belgian.'

'Jules Romain.' Wilde held out his hand, and O'Dowd
shook it. 'I may as well tell the truth. I have spent the last
month in England. I got drowsy, and forgot which side of
the road was which, on the continent.'

'In this mist,' O'Dowd said, 'that could be deadly. With
men like Pierre rushing up and down, eh, Pierre? That car
will not drive again for a while.'

'It will have to be towed away,' Pierre said gloomily.

'And where were you going in such a hurry, my friend?'
O'Dowd asked.

'Well, actually, I thought I'd go into Medoc itself,'
Wilde said. 'But I wanted to drive along by the river, first.'

'Ah, well,' O'Dowd said. 'I think the best thing is for you
to ride with me, Mr. Romain. I do not live far from here,
in the village of Dort. And I have a telephone. You will
come and lunch with me, and we will telephone Bordeaux,
and arrange for another car for you. And for this one to be

picked up.' He smiled at Wilde. 'Does that not sound the best idea?'

(ii)

Wilde scratched his head. 'You really are too kind, Mr. . . . ?'

'O'Dowd. Robert O'Dowd. Now come along, or we will be late for lunch. It is all right, Pierre. I will see to the car. And to this gentleman.'

'As you say, Mr. O'Dowd.' Pierre touched his cap, gazed at the Simca once again. 'Mad,' he said. 'Just crazy. In this mist.' He climbed into his cabin, grated gears.

'You have a bag?' O'Dowd asked. 'I will get it. You must be shaken up.' He wrestled with the Simca's back door, pulled it open, bent down to reach inside. Wilde stood behind him, gazed at the unprotected neck, his mind a jumbling chaos.

'Did you say *Robert* O'Dowd?' he asked.

'That's me,' O'Dowd agreed, and straightened, the overnight bag in his hand. 'You almost sounded as if you had heard my name, before.' He stared at Wilde for a moment. 'But I do not think we have met.'

'We haven't,' Wilde said. 'I did know someone named O'Dowd, once, but his first name wasn't Robert.'

'Get in, get in,' Robert O'Dowd invited. 'We must not be late for lunch. Mama is very insistent that we are punctual.'

Wilde sat down, looked at his hands. They trembled, very slightly. He had killed the wrong man, once before in his career. But then the victim had been a deliberate substitute, no doubt fully aware of the risks he ran.

Robert O'Dowd smiled, opened the glove compartment. 'Brandy? It is a strange feeling, to have come face to face with death, and have survived.'

'I'll manage,' Wilde said.

O'Dowd re-started his engine. 'This other O'Dowd, what was his name?'

The Mercedes purred along the road. 'I once knew a Charles O'Dowd,' Wilde said.

'Did you now?' Robert O'Dowd seemed delighted. 'But that would be Papa.'

Wilde glanced at him. Robert O'Dowd could not be a day under forty.

'Probably just a coincidence,' he said. 'I have never been in the Medoc, before.'

'Ah, but Papa is widely travelled. Or he was once, when he was younger. Now, well, of course, he prefers to stay at home. We do the travelling for him.'

'We?' Wilde asked. The car clung to the road with effortless power, yet the whole of France was turning upside down.

'My brothers and myself. We look after the selling side of the business, you understand, while Papa stays at home, and counts the money. He is very fond of counting money.'

'What business are you in?' Wilde asked.

'What business can anyone be in, in the Gironde?' Robert O'Dowd asked. 'We are wine growers. The whole of Dort is really just our vineyard. Without us, there would be no village. My ancestors settled here three hundred years ago, and started to grow wine. We are of Irish descent, of course. My great-grandfather, to the thirteenth time, was an officer in the English army, but then there was that trouble at the Boyne, and he followed King James into exile. He fought with Berwick for years, until he grew old, and then he settled here on the banks of the Gironde, and planted grapes. Only for his own cellar, then, you understand. For the next century soldiering was our tradition. There was an O'Dowd at Fontenoy, and two of my ancestors were generals under Napoleon the First. An O'Dowd died at Waterloo. On the French side, of course. But after the second abdication, why, the then O'Dowd began selling his wines. Times were hard, you understand. Since then the emphasis has changed. Now we grow wine for a profession, and soldier for a hobby.'

'But you still soldier.'

Robert O'Dowd shrugged. 'Every Frenchman is a soldier, Mr. Romain. My brothers and I have done our service. I will confess to you that we have never fought in a war. That is our good fortune, perhaps.'

'And wine growing involves a great deal of travelling? You seemed an old friend of the girl at the airport.'

'I always leave my keys with her when I am away. Oh, yes, we market Château Dort, as well as grow it. Germany, Italy, England, Scandinavia, the United States . . .' Robert O'Dowd smiled. 'Do you know, we even sell our wine in Eastern Europe? And the Soviet Union. And Asia. There is our greatest triumph, up to now.'

Wilde gazed through the window. They were approaching houses, a cluster of stone cottages, gathered on either side of a pension, facing a very old dock which thrust into the swirling brown water. The tide was rising, at eleven in the morning of the 21st. Just over half tide up, Wilde estimated. So, he did a hasty calculation, it figured; at oh four hundred on the 23rd it would just have turned, as Lucinda had promised, and it would be possible to carry it right out into the bay. The other bank was lost in the mist, and but for the colour of the water, this could have been the sea already. His only remaining problem was a sudden wealth of O'Dowds.

'How many brothers have you?' he asked.

'Ah, there are only four of us, now. Françoise, and my two brothers.'

'Now?'

'Peter was killed, two months ago. A motor accident. Very like yours, just now. But you were lucky.' He glanced at Wilde. 'It would be best not to speak of it, you understand. Especially to Madeleine.'

'Your mother?'

'Oh, no, no. Madeleine was Peter's fiancée. They were to be married, in the New Year. She still feels strongly about it. Well, so do we all. It is not a subject we discuss.'

'I'm sorry,' Wilde said. 'I did not mean . . .'

'But you did not know,' Robert O'Dowd said. 'So there is nothing to be sorry about.'

They had driven through the village, and now turned between huge stone pillars. The drive wound past an orchard of trees, mistily bare, and the château waited in front of them. Nor was the word quite as much of an exaggeration as usual, Wilde realised. Wide double staircases led up to a patio as big as a football pitch, and the house stood behind, a gothic giant of arches and spires, mullioned windows and smoking chimney pots.

'It is the original,' Robert O'Dowd said.

'It is very beautiful,' Wilde agreed.

'It cannot compare with the castles of North Germany,' O'Dowd said. 'But it is certainly old. It is also a battle to keep out the rot. But then, all life is a battle, is it not? Ah, Armand. You are looking well.'

An elderly man had appeared round the corner of the man-made mountain which supported the château; he wore a fishing smock and leggings. 'As are you, Monsieur Robert. As are you. We expected you an hour ago.'

'I was delayed. This is Mr. Romain.'

'Welcome to Dort, Mr. Romain.' Armand got behind the wheel. 'I will see to your bags.'

'The garages are at the side,' Robert O'Dowd said, and led Wilde up the steps. 'I should not really sound disparaging about my home. It *is* my home, and I love it dearly. I would not choose to live anywhere else in the world.'

He was utterly relaxed, utterly confident, utterly at ease. And why should he not be? Wilde wondered. He was a successful wine-merchant, returning from a business trip. Only his name was important. His name, and the fact that he *had* been on a business trip. But Kevin Walner had been killed a week ago. Was that relevant? Would his assassin come straight home? How much simpler to use a business trip as a cover for an assassination.

Except that Robert was not the only O'Dowd around.

And there was no proof. An executioner, in search of a victim, and finding four. Or five? Or more?

'Robert!' She came running across the patio, a girl of perhaps seventeen, Wilde estimated, tall like her brother, wearing riding breeches and a silk shirt, black boots, bareheaded, allowing several feet of curling chestnut hair to drift behind her as she moved. That she was Robert's sister was not in question; there was the same small nose and chin, separated by the same grotesquely wide mouth, dominated by the same amused green eyes. She was not a pretty girl, as her brother was not a handsome man, but the warmth of her voice, and, Wilde guessed, of her personality, burst over the morning. And she was going to be a large woman, full-breasted and wide-hipped. He thanked God that she was in every way too large to be the female accessory Lucinda had described. 'We thought you had had an accident.' She arrived in front of them, panting. 'Oh, excuse me.'

'My pleasure, Miss O'Dowd,' Wilde said.

'This is Mr. Jules Romain,' Robert explained. 'And I did not have an accident. He did.'

'Oh?' Her mouth made a huge circle. 'You are not hurt?'

'Only my pride, Miss O'Dowd.'

She shrugged. 'Ah, what is a little accident, when no one is hurt. And you must call me Françoise.' She tucked her arm through his, escorted him towards the front door. 'You have a strange accent.'

'That is because he is not French,' Robert pointed out. 'But Belgian. She likes you, Mr. Romain. So I think we shall all start calling you Jules, because clearly you are going to stay a while.'

'But of course he is going to stay,' Françoise declared. 'Especially now he has no car. And are you not a friend of Robert's?'

'Unfortunately, no,' Wilde said, and was surprised by her frown. 'But your brother very kindly gave me a lift.'

Robert O'Dowd clapped him on the shoulder. 'So now

we are friends, are we not, Jules?' He winked. 'Be careful
of her. She eats men for breakfast. Now, I will go and telephone the car people.'

'I can do that,' Wilde protested.

'Allow me,' Robert said. 'They know me. I will fix it for
you.'

He hurried ahead of them into the house. Françoise came
to a halt, beneath the huge arch of the front door. 'Is that
not a splendid sight, Jules? Did Robert tell you this house
is nearly three hundred years old? Every time I pass here,
I stop, and think to myself of all the people who have passed
this way, the hundreds, the thousands who must have stood
right here. The Emperor himself, once.'

'Napoleon?'

She laughed, a delicious ripple sound. 'The Third. Ah,
well, one cannot always have the very best. Now come and
meet the family. We are both late, Robert and I, because
I too have had an accident. I was thrown.'

'You were not hurt?'

'A bruise.' She turned round to show him the mud-stained
seat of her breeches. 'I cannot show you the mark itself, at
least not until we know each other better. Much better.'
Again the frown. 'Are you sure you never met Robert, before this morning?'

'I'm afraid not.'

The frown cleared, slowly. 'Anyway,' she said. 'Mama will
at least not be angry with me, because I have brought home
you as a prize. Ah, Ney, you have come to greet my friend?
Where is Soult? Soult? Here, boy.'

The two dachshunds came galloping out of the rear of the
hall, surrounded Wilde, sniffing his legs. One growled.
'Ney!' Françoise commanded. 'Stop that. That is very strange,
Jules. They are usually far too friendly, to strangers. But
they will get used to you. Now, let us hurry.' She seized
his hand, turned off the entry hall to her left, into an enormous room, wide if surprisingly low ceilinged, clearly the
Great Hall of the original house, now occupied mainly by a

large dining table, already set, and on which a maid was placing bottles of red wine.

'Oh, Mademoiselle Françoise,' she said. 'You gave me a start. But your mother is waiting.'

'I have a reason,' Françoise dropped her voice to a whisper. 'I have made a catch, eh? Is he not splendid, Aimee?'

The maid gazed at Wilde, made a half-curtsy, giggled, and hurried from the room.

'I don't think she approves of me,' Wilde said.

'It is I of whom she does not approve,' Françoise promised him, and hurried to the staircase in the next little hall, leading him up and into the main drawing room, where five people were sitting, drinking Pernod. 'Mama!' she cried. 'Mama! A visitor. Mr. Jules Romain.'

Introducing, on my left, the hawk, and on my right, the chickens, Wilde thought. Or was it, on my left, the hare, and on my right, the hounds. Perhaps, somewhere in this house, there was the chicken he wanted; but he had no doubt at all that collectively this family would prove to be a pack of hounds.

Françoise was dragging him forward again. 'This is Mama. Jules Romain, Mama.'

Charles O'Dowd had married well, a long time ago. Even at, say, sixty, his wife was a strikingly handsome woman, tall and strongly built, with prominent chin and cheekbones, a long, straight nose, once red hair, now heavily streaked with grey, but still curly and still worn long, although swept up on top of her head in an untidy crown. 'You are welcome, Mr. Romain,' she said. 'We do not often have visitors to Dort in December.' Her eyes were green.

'Jules is from Ostend,' Françoise explained. 'Papa!'

It was the misfortune of the O'Dowd children, Wilde concluded, collectively to take after their father, except for their eyes, and in Françoise's case, her hair. But Charles O'Dowd could at least be immediately ruled out as the man

who had killed Kevin Walner; Wilde estimated his age as
pushing eighty. He was tall and thin, had the same small
features and big mouth he had bequeathed to his children,
and the same soft voice. His head was a mass of white hair,
and his eyes were a docile brown. They were sad eyes, the
saddest eyes, Wilde realised, that he had seen in a long
time. But this man was still mourning a son. Unlike his
wife?

Charles O'Dowd rose to meet his guest, moving with infinite care. 'Ostend. It is years since I was in Ostend, but I
remember it well. I have always said that Ostend Cathe-
dral is the most beautiful in Europe.'

'Oh, Papa,' Françoise said, frowning. The rest of the
family exchanged glances. Wilde realised that, for some
reason, this old man was an embarrassment to his own
children.

But not to Robert. He came in now, threw his arm round
his father's shoulders; there was genuine affection in the
squeeze. 'You could just be right, Papa. Now, Jules, have
you met my brothers? Jack? Maurice?'

Wilde shook hands. Maurice and Jack were the younger
brothers, apparently, both in their early thirties, very like
Robert in looks. But Jack O'Dowd had a tenseness which
was lacking in the others. His fingers were never still;
neither were his eyes. His handshake was perfunctory.
Someone to think about. Maurice, on the other hand, was
a younger edition of Robert, except that he was also
apparently, the family dandy; he wore a high-collared
double-breasted dark blue jacket over pale red corduroy
trousers, and a red and blue cravat instead of a tie. There
was no trace of hostility in either of their greetings.

'And *this*,' Robert said, 'is Madeleine.'

Wilde dropped his gaze. In the midst of the tall O'Dowds,
here was the child. Except that, age apart, she was clearly
older than any of her hosts, in experience, in feeling. Her
eyes were amber, large, and infinitely sad. They gazed at

him from beneath a slight frown, which he thought might
be permanent, either from worry or short-sightedness. But
not even the frown could affect her beauty. She had deep
yellow hair, which waved, and which she wore to her
shoulders, carefully set so as to curl where it touched. Her
nose was small, her chin pointed, as was her mouth. But in
a generally small face the features fitted together to compose
an almost flawless picture. It was an eighteenth-century face,
and as such, belonged in an eighteenth-century setting like
this house, these surroundings. Far more so, indeed, than
the O'Dowds themselves.

She was hardly more than five feet tall, and thin. Her
dress was a very simple dark green affair, and she wore low-
heeled sandals. Her age was unthinkable. The body of a
twelve-year-old girl, the mind, he suspected of a very old
woman. And she, he realised, the only non-O'Dowd in the
room apart from himself, was alone unhappy at his presence.

(iii)

They lunched, on strawberries from the deep freeze, as was
most of the salad, on ham followed by chops, on an enormous bowl of fruit, on real coffee and Havana cigars. They
drank unlabelled wine which had a bouquet matching any
Wilde had ever sampled. They chatted, in the gayest of
moods.

'He pulled out!' Robert cried. 'In the mist. Ah, he is a
crazy driver, this Jules.'

'And it was Pierre?' Maurice demanded. 'That madman?'

'With a truckload of Dort wine, if you please.' Robert
laughed. 'Had they hit, what a catastrophe.'

'He means, you see, Jules,' Jack explained, 'that the possible loss of your life, and Pierre's, oh, that would be
nothing. But a truckload of Dort wine, that would be a
crime.'

'That would be murder,' Robert declared. 'But all is well

that ends well, eh? And you know what caused the trouble?
The English, as usual. Oh, yes. Tell them, Jules.'

'Well,' Wilde said. 'I have spent such a long time in
England, recently, on business, that I have got used to
driving on the wrong side of the road, and this morning I
forgot where I was.'

'But no matter, no matter,' Charles O'Dowd said. 'As
Robert says, it has ended without trouble. And they will
send a fresh car out for you, I am sure.'

'But where do you go, Mr. Romain, in the Medoc in
December?' Mrs. O'Dowd asked.

'Well,' Wilde said, 'I finished my business a few days
early, in England, and so I thought I would take a plane
down here. You know, I have travelled all over Western
Europe for my firm, all over France, and yet, strangely,
never the Medoc. And believe me, Mrs. O'Dowd, I appre-
ciate good wines.'

'Then you are doubly welcome,' Charles O'Dowd said.
'And there is no better place for claret than Dort. Robert
says you were going on to Medoc itself? What nonsense.
You will spend the night here, Mr. Romain, and this afternoon the boys will show you what they can. I say what they
can, because obviously December is not a good time to see
the industry. But no doubt you will find it interesting
enough.'

'Oh, I could not possibly . . .'

'We should like you to spend the night,' Robert O'Dowd
said. Remarkably, he was looking not at Wilde, but at his
mother.

'You are a traveller, Jules?' Françoise sat on his right.
She had selected the place herself. 'In what line?'

'Cosmetics,' Wilde decided.

'Ooh!' she squealed. 'You have samples?'

'I'm afraid I sent them home. I have only my clothes with
me.'

'Oh.' She was disappointed. 'But perhaps you will be able
to tell me about them. I know. I will show you all of mine,

and you will tell me which are good, and which are bad.'

'My pleasure,' Wilde said. Now, what on earth had made him choose cosmetics?

'I find it strange,' Madeleine's voice was very low. 'Christmas is on Sunday. You have finished your work early, and yet instead of hurrying home, you visit a strange place. Have you no home, Mr. Romain?' Her gaze shrouded him, suspicious, and yet . . . he could not decide on the other emotion.

'Well, as a matter of fact, my only home is my apartment in Ostend,' he agreed. 'I have no family, you see, and Christmas is above all a time for families, so I prefer to be on the road, travelling. Until this morning, I was actually regretting that I had finished my work early.'

'But how terrible!' Françoise cried. 'To be alone at Christmas.'

'Yes, of course,' Madeleine agreed. 'Mama, shall we not invite Mr. Romain to spend the rest of the week here?'

'Oh, *could* we, Mama?' Françoise cried.

'I think that would be a splendid idea, Mama,' Robert said.

'But of course you must stay, Mr. Romain,' Mrs. O'Dowd said. 'If you will not be bored.'

'I am overwhelmed by your generosity, Mrs. O'Dowd,' Wilde said. 'By all of your generosity. But I do not see how you can let a stranger interfere with your Christmas celebrations.'

'What nonsense!' Françoise shouted. "You are a Christmas present. To us all. And you will not be bored. I will see to that. Are you finished, Jules? Then come with me. Oh, bring your cigar.'

She held his hand, dragged him out of the dining room and back up the stairs, along a brief corridor into the gallery at the back of the house. She gestured at the paintings. 'O'Dowds. All of them. Painted on their twenty-first birthdays. It is a family tradition. I will join them, eventually.'

O'Dowds had always looked like O'Dowds, Wilde

decided, walking slowly down the room. 'Which one is Peter?'

'There.'

Peter O'Dowd, oddly enough, was an exception to the rule, and looked like his mother.

'He died in October,' Françoise said, and sighed.

'I know,' Wilde said. 'Robert told me about it. I'm sorry.'

'He was a treasure,' Françoise said, and sighed.

Madeleine hung beside him, Wilde realised. He had not recognised her, at first glance. The girl in the picture was laughing, eyes twinkling, lovely face dissolved in happiness. A sister to the present Madeleine. A sister who had never known unhappiness. Then.

'But they were not married?' he asked.

'Oh, no. She was his mistress, of course.' Françoise flushed. 'They were so much in love. That is why Mama said her portrait must hang here.'

'She lives with you?'

'She has an apartment in Paris. But like you, she has no family. So she spends Christmas with us. I think Mama would like to adopt her, have her here all the time. She is beautiful, is she not? Still. Although Mama says that unless she learns how to smile again, she will soon lose her looks. Which would be a tragedy. Now here,' she threw open a window, to allow a blast of icy air to combat the heat in the room. 'Here is the garden. It looks dreadful, now, but in the spring . . . you should see it then.'

Wilde stood at her shoulder. A wide gravel path led from the rear of the patio, towards a distant fountain, and side paths radiated off like the spokes of a wheel. The soil in the beds was freshly turned, every plant was pruned back virtually to its stem. Mainly roses, he estimated. The O'Dowds were enthusiastic gardeners. But then, they were enthusiastic about everything they did. How could such enthusiasm for life include a willingness to take other lives? So perhaps any of the three brothers filled the nebulous description offered by Mrs. Walner, just as the woman Madeleine could have been the woman at the Walner house. Perhaps. This was a job for a detective, not an executioner. Executioners came later, when proof was there. Never in his life had he felt such peace, such an excitement at being alive, such a pleasure in the sheer business of drawing breath.

Françoise turned, in his arms, stood on tiptoe, kissed him on the lips.

'Did your mother never tell you to beware of strangers?'

'There are strangers,' she said seriously, 'and strangers. Besides, you are not a stranger. I told you. You are my Christmas present. And even more besides, you are a cosmetic salesman. What is the most important thing about a lipstick? Surely its taste. You must tell me how mine tastes.'

'I'm not sure I can afford an opinion, on such a brief acquaintance.'

She laughed. It was a sound he would never forget. 'Then you must get to know it better.' This time her arms went round his neck, her tongue searched his, her body worked against his. She was like a bitch puppy, eager and anxious, hot and sweaty from her morning's ride and the wine she had drunk at lunch, surely in love with life, with the business of living.

But it was impossible to prevent himself responding. How long was it since he had held an innocent teenage girl in his arms? In his business the women either belonged, and were therefore to be treated with suspicion, or they belonged nowhere at all, and were strictly disposable.

'Oh, Jules,' she whispered. 'You *are* my Christmas present. Are you not superstitious? I am. I dreamed that a man would come to Dort.' She smiled at him, and there were tears in her eyes. 'Uninvited. Unsuspecting. And he spoke with a foreign accent. Do you know, I thought it was a nightmare, and could not sleep again? But when I saw you this morning, I thought to myself, he can be no nightmare. Oh, Jules.'

'On the other hand,' Wilde said. 'I *am* a stranger,

Françoise. And twice your age. I'm not sure your mother
would approve.' He disengaged himself as Robert O'Dowd
entered the room.

'Oh, there you are, Jules. If you wish, I will take you
down to the village, and show you something of our business. As Papa says, there is little enough to see, at this
moment, but you might like to take a look.'

'I should enjoy that very much,' Wilde said.

'And I shall come too,' Françoise announced.

Robert raised his eyes, and shrugged. 'You see how it is,
Jules. She is an afterthought. You know, thirteen years
younger than Maurice. So she rules us with a rod of iron.
But you will wish to wash your hands and change your
clothes. Shall we say, half an hour? And you leave the man
alone, Françoise. Until then, at any rate.'

Wilde winked at the girl, followed Robert into a long
corridor at the far end of the gallery. 'This is your room,'
Robert O'Dowd said. 'Your bag has been brought up. Half
an hour.' He continued along the corridor.

Wilde turned the handle. The room was the second away
from the gallery. He wondered whose was the one in between. Another guest room, probably. Certainly he hoped
it did not belong to Françoise. That young lady was going
to be a problem. The whole family was already a problem.
An absurd problem. A problem which could be solved
merely by relaxing for the rest of today, and leaving first
thing tomorrow morning, for Sete and the boat. Why
should he lose any sleep? He had already deposited the
fifteen thousand dollars in one of the many safe deposits
he kept scattered throughout England and Western Europe.
Sir Gerald was never so trusting; he always paid half down
and half on completion.

So did he then, perform his duties only for the cash?
It was possible that one of these happy, confident, wealthy,
secure brothers was a cold-blooded assassin. It was *possible*.

He closed the door behind him, frowned. Once again he
had been far away when he entered the room. His pre-

occupation was indeed becoming dangerous. But his senses were still those highly trained antennae they had always been. His overnight bag lay on his bed, closed. But would Armand or whichever of the servants had brought it up have put it on the bed? And there was a scent in the room. The faintest of perfumes. Yet the room was empty.

How empty is empty? He skirted the wall, moving sideways to watch the rest of the room, the wardrobe, while he reached the bathroom door, threw it open. That was empty. He closed it again, opened the wardrobe door. This also appeared to be empty, but now his nostrils clouded with scent. He had smelt it first at lunch, no, just before lunch, faint in the midst of so many other scents. He thrust his hand to the left, into the dark recess at the side of the wardrobe, closed it on soft flesh, drew out Madeleine.

5

'PARDON me,' Wilde said. 'I thought it was a mouse.'

There was a slight flush in her cheeks, nothing more. Her left hand came up to rub her shoulder. 'You have very powerful fingers, Mr. Romain.'

'Jules,' he said. 'The family has decided to call me Jules, remember?'

'I do not belong to this family, Mr. Romain. Now, if you will excuse me . . .'

'You're not leaving? I was hoping this was a social call.'

'I wanted to see that you were comfortable.'

'Well, just hold on a moment, will you? I haven't found out yet.' He lay on the bed, hands beneath head, gazed at her. 'Seems okay. Very soft. But it's a double.'

Her expression never changed. 'You are trying to be rude to me, Mr. Romain.'

'As a matter of fact, yes. You're too good looking to be a
zombie.' He reached down, opened his overnight bag,
flipped the lid upwards. 'Perhaps I interrupted you,
Madeleine. Madeleine Who?'

She came towards the bed, moving slowly across the par-
quet floor, and noiselessly, too, he realised. 'My name is
Corot. I am not related to the artist. Now tell me why you
have come to Dort?'

'Is it important?'

'Yes,' she said. 'If it is not important that you came here,
Mr. Romain, and important that you stay, then it is very
important that you leave. Soon. Now. This very afternoon.
You came, uninvited. Leave the same way. The hire company will deliver a car for you this afternoon. Take it and
go, when no one is around.'

'I don't really see how I can do that, darling,' Wilde
said. 'I've been invited to stay. By you amongst others. I like
the place. I like the people. I even like you. Besides, it would
be rude.'

Her tongue came out, flicked her lips. Then she shrugged,
very faintly. 'You are a fool.' She turned away from the bed.

'Tell me,' Wilde said. 'Whom were you expecting, Miss
Corot?'

She checked, but did not turn her head. 'I expect no one.'

'Mistakes on both sides,' Wilde said pleasantly. But suddenly he was angry. She had ruined his day, his afternoon,
his anticipations, his half-formed decision. She had taken
his scepticism and rolled it into a ball, and thrown it out of
the window. Now, why had she done that?

Still she hesitated. 'One word, Mr. Romain. You will tell
no one that I was here?'

She was a fly, caught in the web. Out of her own
curiosity, or something more than that? Wilde swung his
legs off the bed. 'They wouldn't approve?'

She shook her head. 'In some ways they are very old-
fashioned.'

'So explain Françoise.'

'Françoise is Françoise. There is only one rule that Françoise must not break, the rule of knowledge. They regard me differently.'

He held her shoulders, gently this time, turned her round. She gazed at him, her beautiful face a mask of solemnity, the faint frown lines gathered between her eyes. 'So in your spare time,' he said, very softly, 'you write anonymous letters.'

(ii)

The colour was back in her cheeks. 'I do not understand you,' she whispered.

'The feeling is mutual, darling, believe me,' Wilde said. 'But I'm going to try, very hard. And if you don't cooperate, you may discover that I have some *very* unpleasant characteristics.'

He held her arm, gently urged her back towards the bed, made her sit. Her face was pale again, but she was terrified. At what she had done, now coming home to roost? He figured she had a lot of talking to do.

'I do not understand,' she said again. 'Anything. I . . .' She sprang to her feet as the door opened.

'Jules?' Robert O'Dowd asked. 'All ready?' He frowned. 'Madeleine?'

Now the pale face was aflame. 'I . . . I . . . I . . .'

'I asked her to come in, old man,' Wilde said. 'To be frank, I wanted her to give me a few tips on wine, so I wouldn't appear to be a complete ignoramus.'

Robert O'Dowd's frown slowly cleared. 'You Belgians,' he said. 'I think Mama is looking for you, Madeleine.'

'Yes,' she said. 'Yes. I must go to her.' She brushed past him, hurried down the corridor.

'My car is waiting,' Robert O'Dowd said. 'So is Françoise.'

'I'm on my way,' Wilde said. 'I have not offended you, I hope, Robert?'

'Of course not, Jules. It is just that, well, down here in the south, I suppose we do not have the sophistication of the Parisians. Or of the Belgians, perhaps. A woman, alone in a man's bedroom . . . it would cause a great scandal, were the servants to get hold of it.'

'I'm most terribly sorry,' Wilde said. 'Yes, as you say, I am too used to the big cities. But you say Paris? Pouf. You have not been to London, recently. That I can tell.'

Robert O'Dowd led him into the corridor. 'No,' he said. 'I have no use for London. I have little use for the English at all.' He smiled over his shoulder. 'It is my Irish blood, I imagine.'

'London,' Wilde said. 'It is the sin capital of the world. It is so sinful that there is no sin. Not to find a girl in a man's bedroom, there is the sin, in London. The sin of foolishness. I imagine your younger brothers find it interesting enough.'

'You must ask them,' Robert O'Dowd said. 'I must confess that we travel mostly on business. For relaxation we prefer to sail. Here, on the Gironde, or a little farther north, on the Golden Coast. Do you do much sailing, Jules?'

'But of course,' Wilde said. 'I live in Ostend.'

'Ah, the North Sea. Give me Biscay, any time.' They had descended a second staircase, at the far end of the corridor and at the opposite end of the house to the gallery. Here they emerged into the entry hall, just as a car horn blared. 'Françoise is very impatient,' Robert O'Dowd said. 'She is also very young, very inexperienced, totally unsophisticated. I say these things as a friend, Jules. And I know you will take them in the same spirit.'

He walked ahead, to the steps. Wilde gazed at the broad shoulders, the thin neck, the flapping fair hair. What had Madeleine Corot been going to say? Would she ever say anything, now? Would she be allowed to? Even if the men in the family were prepared to take him at face value, the mere fact that they had something to hide, and that she had been alone with him, would be upsetting enough. But he had to speak with her again.

He looked up at the cloudless blue sky, the pale December sun. It was even mild. What a thoroughly lousy afternoon.

'There is room for us all in the front,' Françoise said, and moved into the middle. Wilde sat beside her, and her arm went round his waist. 'Oh, don't open the window,' she protested. 'We'll freeze.'

Wilde subsided, allowed himself to be cuddled. Robert O'Dowd sat on her other side, turned the car on to the drive. 'Have you ever tasted Château Dort?' he asked.

'I'm afraid not. I'm a very ignorant man about wines. Is it called Château after the house?'

'Well, not entirely, you know. The wine-growing areas of the Gironde are divided into communes, and each wine takes its name from the centre of the commune, so ours is named Dort. It is one of the smallest communes. But I may say that there are only about two dozen better clarets available.'

'Two dozen? You're very modest.'

Robert O'Dowd smiled. 'It is not modesty, Jules. That has nothing to do with it. The production of wines and their subsequent classification, is an exact science. In the first place, you see, all the wines of this district are divided into what we call "growths"; the exact word is "cru". The ones of which you will have heard, and perhaps tasted, are all "classed growths", that is, claret, as opposed to the bourgeois or peasant growths. And then, the classed growths themselves are subdivided into first growth, second growth, and so on, down to the fifth growth. You think of a first-class growth, well, there are only three, the Lafite, the Margaux, and the Latour. There are many more in the second and third growths, of course. Dort is a third growth. So therefore it must be recognised that any wine in the second and first growth is possibly better.'

'A class system at its very worst,' Wilde said. 'Who decides which is in what growth?'

'It was first done at a conference of wine-brokers in 1855,' Robert O'Dowd explained. 'But of course their judgement

was based upon many, many years of experience. Oh, they
took records of wines well back into the eighteenth century.
And it is not at all arbitrary, you know, Jules. Oh, no, no.
The quality of wine does not really depend on the grape,
not even on the methods of cultivation or production, but
on the soil in which the grape is grown. Here in the Gironde,
we have many different varieties of soil, which is why we can
produce so many different varieties of wine. But our secret,
our truly great secret, is a layer of a peculiar kind of stone
which exists in certain areas here in the Medoc, and which
we call *alios*. Sometimes it is hard, sometimes it is even a
little spongy. Generally it lies about two or three feet under
the surface. It is found extensively, for example, around
Pauillac. So it is not a coincidence that the Lafite and the
Latour are Pauillac growths. It is possible to say that they
are the two finest red wines in the world.'

'The Latour was recommended to me in London,' Wilde
murmured, and watched the Gironde rushing past on his
left. It was just on three in the afternoon, and as clear as it
was likely to become, but the mist still clung thinly to the
water. The tide was falling now, bubbling downriver at
almost the same speed as it had risen; he remembered from
his voyage in *Regina B,* in September, that it was not a tide
to miss, in either direction. 'The '44.'

'Oh, yes, in London,' Robert O'Dowd agreed. 'It will cost
you five pounds a bottle, and unless you have an educated
palate, any other Pauillac wine will taste just as good.' He
pulled off the road next to the dock, got out and stretched
his legs. 'It is most remarkably mild, for mid-December. It
could almost be spring.'

Françoise at last managed to release Wilde, ran on to the
creaking dock, her hands clasped at her throat. 'Isn't it won-
derful, Jules? I love this river, and yet I am terrified of it.
It is so fast. And always there is the mist. I think, if I ever
decide to commit suicide, it will have to be in the Gironde.'

'What a macabre thought,' Wilde said.

'Oh, it could happen, Jules. I am very emotional. I could

easily be crossed in love. And then, if I died in the river, I'd be reunited with Peter. He drowned, only a few miles up from here. His car went into the river, you know.'

Wilde glanced at Robert. And at lunch they had joked about another near miss.

'We will have a cognac with Pierre, first,' Robert O'Dowd said.

Françoise seized Wilde's hand, imprisoned her own between his fingers. 'Although perhaps it would be better to drown myself in wine. More dramatic, do you not think? That would even be reported in the Paris newspapers.'

They walked across the road. A dog sat up and gazed at them, and a cat turned over and went back to sleep. A curtain moved in an upstairs window of the house, beside the pension. But on a winter's afternoon there was no reason for anyone to be out of doors.

Robert O'Dowd opened the front door of the pension, went into the little bar. 'Pierre? Pierre? Is Pierre back yet, madame?'

'I am here, Mr. Robert.' Pierre came bustling out of the back, drying his hands on a towel. 'I am preparing a specialty.'

'For us, Pierre?' Françoise squeezed Wilde's hand.

'Oh, you are welcome, mademoiselle. But it is for our guest. Did you not know that we had a guest?' Pierre dropped his voice to a whisper, leaned over the bar. 'He arrived yesterday morning. By taxi, if you please.'

They gazed through the bead curtain behind the bar at the restaurant, where Pierre's guest was lingering over a late lunch, smoking a pipe and reading a newspaper. The newspaper had moved as their heads had turned. Wilde wondered what it was in their psychology that made policemen, even when separated by nationality and by training, cultivate the same habits. But what had brought *him* to Dort?

'You are fortunate. We will have a glass of cognac,' Robert O'Dowd said, turning his back on the man in the other room. 'And a Dubonnet for mademoiselle.'

'He treats me like a child,' Françoise complained, and stood on tiptoe to kiss Wilde on the cheek. 'And he does not like me to be affectionate.'

'I am sure you are causing Jules a great deal of embarrassment. Pour yourself one as well, Pierre.' He brushed his glass against Wilde's. 'Your health. Now, tell me, Pierre, you delivered the load?'

'Oh, yes, Mr. Robert. All safely.'

'When you came back, was Mr. Romain's car still there?'

'Ah,' Pierre said, looking lugubrious. 'Yes, Mr. Robert. And there was a policeman there, too. Very sad. After all, it was a private matter. Nobody was hurt.'

'I expect he just happened along,' Robert O'Dowd said.

'Do you think they've a warrant out for my arrest?' Wilde asked.

Robert O'Dowd did not seem amused. 'Of course not, Jules. They may come to the house and ask questions, that is all. But you let me talk to them.' He finished his drink. 'We will go through the back, Pierre.' He parted the curtain, nodded to the detective, and also to madame, who was at that moment bustling out of the kitchen with a fresh bottle of wine. 'Remarkable,' he said. 'Not one, but two strangers, coming to Dort, in December. That is very unusual, eh, Françoise?'

'I didn't like that one,' Françoise said in the privacy of the kitchen. 'Did you see his eyes? They looked at us, at me, anyway, all the way, up and down, and when I looked back, he looked away. I mean, I like to be admired by men, but if they look away when I look at them, then I think their thoughts must have been dirty. Do you not agree, Jules?'

'Oh, every time.' Wilde decided it was time to get back on to a safe subject. 'What was the basis on which the division into growths was made?'

'Ah, well, there are a great many factors, you know.' Robert O'Dowd opened a mildewed door set in a crumbling stone wall, and led them back into the open air. The whole of the second street of Dort was composed of a row of small warehouses, each house connected to its neighbour by a low passageway. 'It depends on things such as the amount of alcohol in the wine, the acidity, the amount of tartaric acid, the sugar content, the glycerin content, and the amount of extract. It varies a great deal, and of course, no wine in memory has ever had the *perfect* combination of virtues. But one year, one year, Jules, it must happen. That is surely a natural law. I hope I am still alive to see it.'

'I'll drink to that,' Wilde agreed. 'But what I cannot understand, Robert, is why your wine is not ranked as good as the Pauillac. You are only a few miles away.'

'Not enough *alios*,' Robert said. 'It is as simple as that.' He unlocked a door in the first warehouse, to admit them into a large cellar, filled from floor to ceiling with hogsheads. The smell was enough to make a drunkard happy for eternity; Wilde filled his lungs and wondered why anyone ever wasted his time drinking the stuff, which involved buying it, when he could just come in here and have a sniff. 'Our wealth, in its most basic state.' But Robert O'Dowd was frowning, no longer urbane. So he could recognise a policeman as well as anyone.

'Where's the press?' Wilde asked. 'My conception of wine making is of a huge vat with a lot of happy fellows trampling round and round, squashing the grapes and singing.'

Françoise gave a peal of laughter.

'We do not press our grapes like that,' Robert said. 'They are just piled into the vat, and their own weight expels the liquid. That is far and away the best method.'

'Good heavens,' Wilde said.

'But there is the press, over there,' Robert said. 'You'll see it is mechanically operated. Now in these hogsheads are the current crop, harvested in October, as I said. The must is accumulated in barrels, and allowed to ferment, for a period of ten days, you know.'

'The must?'

'It is the name we use for the raw grape juice.'

'Oh, I see. So after harvesting, you just let it squash itself flat, bung it into barrels, add a bit of yeast, and sit back with saliva dripping from your mouth.'

Robert O'Dowd smiled. 'It is even simpler than that, Jules. We never add yeast. This is wine, not beer, we are making. This is claret. There is the yeast germ already present in the grape, and this is all that is required. Well, as I was saying, this young wine completed its first fermentation over a month ago, and *then* the must was pressed, before it was drawn into these hogsheads here. Of course, the first fermentation removed nearly all the sugar, but the second, the long fermentation, is the really important one. It is in the middle of this process now. It should be ready for racking by the end of February.'

'Racking? Oh, you mean bottling?'

'You cannot bottle a good wine for at least two years, my friend. You see, this young wine is so full of sediment and foreign matter that it is quite undrinkable.' He removed a cup from the hook on the wall, lifted out the bung from the nearest hogshead, and dipped. The liquid looked like dark red mud. 'You see?' Robert O'Dowd threw it on the floor.

'What is that peculiar thing under the bung?' Wilde asked.

'It is a special seal, which allows gas to escape from the cask, but does not allow air to flow back in. This is important. I have just set this cask back at least a week.' He did not seem worried, about that. 'Now, racking merely means getting rid of the sediment. We do this about six times in all, with a good year's harvest. It is done at intervals of about three months at first, and then six-monthly intervals during the final year. In here, for instance,' he led them through the low corridor into the next cellar, 'is last year's harvest, which has already been racked twice. And in the next cellar is the year before's, which is very nearly ready for bottling.' He unlocked another door. 'It's a long business.'

'And once the racking is finished, that stuff goes on our tables?'

Robert O'Dowd smiled. 'You could serve it then, presumably. But it would still not be a very good wine. To be perfected, you see, it has to be fined. So that it gets that clear, bright colour which is the mark of a good claret. We use the white of egg. It is quite a process.' He knelt in front of a hogshead, a cup in his hand, turned a tap. 'You said you had never tasted Château Dort.'

'Wasn't that your wine at lunch?'

'A peasant growth.' Robert O'Dowd handed him the cup. 'This is not perfect, of course.'

Wilde held the cup to his nostrils. 'Am I doing it right? I should hold it to the light, too, shouldn't I? Difficult, with a cup.'

Robert O'Dowd smiled. 'Drink it, Jules. That is what it is for. Nothing is more amusing than to watch a novice trying to assess a wine by an expert's methods. To you, to ninety-nine per cent of all men, fortunately, wine is for drinking, not comparing.'

Wilde drank, smacked his lips. 'I must say, rather pleasant.'

'It is a good wine,' Robert agreed. 'I am pleasantly surprised with it.'

'The whole thing seems so cut and dried, and simple, I wonder everyone in the Gironde is not a millionaire.'

'Ah, well, you see, each year's crop is subject to so many factors. The soil may be the most important, but the climate, the temperature of the summer, the amount of rainfall, the amount of sunshine, all of these can affect a wine considerably. And then there are diseases which can wipe out an entire crop. Do you know, in 1882 we suffered a disease called phylloxera, which persisted for three years? Not only us, of course; the whole Medoc. As a matter of fact, the output has never recovered. Some would say the quality has never quite recovered, either.'

'I've read a lot about that,' Wilde said. 'Did your family lose a lot of money?'

'Everyone lost a lot of money,' Robert said grimly. 'It is an

all or nothing business.' But his preoccupation was growing all the time. 'I tell you what, Jules, I wish you to return
to the house. Françoise will drive you. I must have a word
with Pierre.'

'About that fellow?'

Robert O'Dowd glanced at him, frowning. 'It is a business matter. You understand, Jules.'

(iii)

Françoise O'Dowd swung the Mercedes, sent it roaring
along the road. She giggled. 'After what happened this
morning, he is afraid to let you drive his car.'

'Very sensible,' Wilde said. 'Tell me, is there no, well,
labour force connected with your cellars? Come to think of
it, the whole village seems deserted.'

'The week before Christmas is always a holiday. They are
all in Bordeaux, shopping. All! We have only four families.
But that is all we need. We import labour for the harvest,
of course. But the rest, pouf, it is simply a matter of top-
ping up the casks as the wine level drops, and Pierre can do
that just as well.'

'You must have needed additional labour when you
replanted,' Wilde suggested. 'When was it, four years
ago?'

'Yes. Oh, it was a terrible time. It was the year after we
had had to rebuild the entire rear of the house, because of
the death watch beetle.' She giggled again. 'Do you know,
Jules, then we were so poor we could not even afford wine
with our meals. But it all worked out.'

'What destroyed the vines? Phylloxera?'

'Oh, no. Oidium.'

'Oidium can be cured by a sulphur spray.'

She glanced at him. 'You *are* knowledgeable, Jules. I
thought you knew nothing of wines? The worst effects can
be avoided, by spraying. But it cannot really be cured.' The

Mercedes swung off the road, bumped over the uneven ground beneath the trees, came to a halt, totally concealed from the road. 'Listen to the wind.'

It was just starting, whispering through the trees. And they were twenty miles from the Bay. Sammy Bennett would be glad to be in Royon, getting ready for his trip upriver tonight. But Wilde did not think he was going to be able to wait for tomorrow night. Whichever of the O'Dowds was his man, there could be no doubt that the other two brothers knew the secret, and the presence of a detective was going to change the situation. But as Lucinda had said, there was a very simple way to determine the man he wanted.

'Your brothers do a great deal of travelling. Do you ever go with them?'

'Oh, not me. They take Madeleine, sometimes. She is the company secretary, you know.'

'But she didn't accompany Robert, on this last trip.'

'Oh, well, I suppose she wasn't necessary. He only went for two days.'

Now, why should that suddenly make the afternoon so much brighter? Because he liked Robert O'Dowd? Certainly. But he had liked other targets, in the past. Because he respected him? True enough. But again, not quite true *enough*. Because he suspected that the urbanity and air of quiet confidence hid a very hard man indeed? And Wilde, past forty, and with Catherine Light on his mind, wanted the easiest opposition he could find? Because there was no longer any zest in the personal confrontation he had always used to preserve his pride?

'Only two days,' he said. 'Strange. I got the impression, perhaps from the way he was welcomed, that he had been away much longer.'

She laughed. 'We are a passionate family, Jules. We do everything with passion. Last week, for instance, both Maurice and Jack were away, and Madeleine, too, and when *they* came back, there was quite a party.'

'Both . . . Do you know, I think we should get back to
the château.'

She took his face between her hands, and kissed him on
the mouth. Her tongue drove at his teeth like waves pounding on a groin, and he allowed it through. Her hands slipped
inside his coat, and his jacket, unbuttoned his shirt to scrape
over his chest, pluck at his nipples. 'We are better here,'
she said. 'We shall not be interrupted.'

'You make very sudden decisions.' But that wasn't true
at all. Her colour was viola purple, and beneath that puppy
exterior there was a permanent state of mind, a permanent
decision.

'Not sudden. Not sudden at all.' She gazed at him, her
face only inches away, her breath mingling with his. 'Do
you not like me?'

'I like you very much.'

'But you will not touch me. You think I am too young.
Oh, I know you must be a great many years older than me.'

'About twenty.'

'Which I think is just the right difference, between a man
and a woman. Perhaps you think I am not a woman. Oh,
you are so wrong.' Her fingers released her cardigan, rippled
down her own shirt front, her hands thrust beneath her
armpits to release her brassière. She took his hands in hers,
guided them to the large, hard breasts—the tumescent
nipples shivered as he touched her—and reached up for his
mouth again. Her anxious innocence was terrifying. Her
sexuality was in itself a cliché, a touch in time, a matter of
feeling, for the moment. But she was, after all, a woman as
she had claimed, with a woman's urges. Her hands were
busy with his belt. 'Oh, Jules, Jules, I told you, I dreamed.
I dreamed, and never saw his face. I had no idea what he
looked like. And because he was faceless, I told you, I
thought he must be evil. I thought it was a nightmare, and
I awoke shivering, and could not go back to sleep.'

Between each word her tongue snaked out, licked his
mouth, his chin, his nose, his eyes. Her nails scoured his

flesh. And her eyes were closed. Despite himself he felt his
hands slipping from her breasts, down to the tight waistband
of her riding breeches. Here there was a single clip, and then
an already sagging zip; the compulsive throbbing of her own
belly would do the rest. And why not take her, take whatever
she offered? For eight months he had been celibate, until
the day before yesterday, because he had fallen in love.
Wilde, the man who had always used women as mere tools,
weaknesses in another man's armour, to be manipulated to
the Eliminator's advantage. He had weakened himself,
attempted to change the habits of a lifetime, not deliberately, but through sheer disinterest in all women save one.
Now his interest was reawakened; he would have had to be
a eunuch for it not to be. And this girl was nothing, to the
Eliminator. He was here to destroy the murderer of Kevin
Walner, and in doing that would surely destroy the whole of
this tightly knit family. After today, after tonight, this girl
would have nothing left. He would have done that to her.
So where was the difference if he destroyed her now?

She rose to her knees, twisting towards him, as his hands
drove downwards, bringing her entire self into his grasp,
yielding a damp world of softness and heat, moaning slightly
as he reached her bruise. She crawled on to his lap, and one
hand left him long enough to release the catch on the seat,
allow it to lie backwards. Now her eyes were open again,
staring into his, and now, before he was even ready for her,
she was his. Forever. If he wanted.

'Jules,' she whispered. 'Oh, Jules. Jules! Take me away
with you, Jules. Take me away from here. I cannot bear to
remain here, a moment longer. I hate the place. I hate
Dort. Take me away.'

She lay on his chest, momentarily exhausted; he could
feel her heart pounding. 'From here, sweetheart? Tell me
why.'

'I just want to go,' she said. 'Away. Anywhere. They will
not let me. I feel I am in a prison. And there is . . . oh, it is
impossible to describe. Yes. You. You are here. Do you know

when last we had a stranger in our house? And you have
been invited to stay. You are unique, Jules. I do not know
why. I suppose Robert likes you. But after you leave again,
there will be no one. Jules . . .'

Her hands were active again. He eased himself out from
beneath her, got into the driving seat. Her hands followed
him. 'Jules!'

'We'll get you home, I think,' he said. 'Before we do something you might regret.'

'No,' she whispered. 'No regrets. Is that not the national
anthem of the new France? No regrets, Jules. I promise.
Jules!'

He fastened button after button, allowed his breathing to
settle down. So his frustrations would make him angry.
Anger was necessary, now. 'You got what you wanted,
sweetheart. Let's leave it at that.'

'No,' she said. 'I wanted you, as well.'

'Why? You're way ahead.'

'You do not understand, Jules. I am not a virgin. There
was a boy, last year. I do not think it was love. It was an
excitement, because I think we were both lonely. We wanted
to do so much, together. But Robert found out, and he made
Albert go away. Since then I have been so lonely, I have
dreamed of Albert, every night. And then, last week, I
dreamed of you. You, Jules.'

'You dreamed of a faceless monstrosity, darling. And believe me, he *was* a nightmare.' He started the engine, found
reverse.

Françoise sat up, arms folded. 'I hate you. You are a
hateful man. You are making fun of me.'

'No,' he said. 'Believe me.'

'Ha,' she said. 'You are afraid of my brothers. It makes
no difference, you know. So you did not take me. But you
still interfered with me. If I were to tell them . . .'

'I would leave,' he said, and parked in front of the steps.

'You are not going to leave, Jules? You are going to stay
for Christmas. You must. You are my present.'

He opened his door. 'If I were you,' he said, 'I'd get dressed. Or there *will* be a scandal.' He got out of the door, climbed the steps, walked across the patio. So he hated himself now, as well. That was nothing new. And hating helped. Hating was essential. It began with himself, could soon be channelled, into his target. Never before had he begun the hate without actually knowing who his target was. There were Americans for you. They were pragmatists. Realists, perhaps. The English were too inclined still to pose, to think in gestures. Lucinda's reasoning was very direct, very simple. There was a killer named O'Dowd to be eliminated, and information pointed to his being in Dort. That the information might have come from a frustrated or distraught young woman was not relevant. It had been sent to the right place, therefore it was to be believed. That she might have sent it to more than one place was also not relevant. That there might be more than one O'Dowd, was not relevant. That one of the O'Dowds might be a hungry, lonely, frightened girl who did not even know of what she was frightened, was not relevant. You employ the best man in the field, the expert, and you tell him to get it done. It was, after all, simply a matter of asking a question, in the right place. So both Maurice and Jack had been away last week. But there had been only one man at the Walner house. And that was all that need interest Wilde. Thank God.

He opened the front door, went inside. The house was silent. It was five o'clock in the afternoon. What did French households do at five o'clock in the afternoon? Certainly they did not have tea. But he could not stay down here. The man-eating flower in the Mercedes would be up at any moment.

He ran up the stairs on the right of the hall, gained the upper corridor, bumped into Aimee, coming towards him with a basket of washing.

'Mr. Romain!' she exclaimed. 'There was a policeman here, earlier, asking for you. A traffic officer.'

'I seemed to have missed him,' Wilde said.

'It is no matter. He will return in the morning. And the hired car company has delivered another car. Armand put it in the garage for you.'

'That was very kind of him. Now will you tell me one more thing, mademoiselle. I wish to have a word with Miss Corot. Can you tell me where she is?'

Her mouth made a round O. 'But she had gone.'

Alarm bells jangled in Wilde's brain. 'Gone? Gone where?'

'She has gone to Paris, monsieur. With Mrs. O'Dowd and Mr. Jack.'

PART TWO

THE SUNLESS LAND

6

THE bells rose to a crescendo. 'When did they go?' Wilde
asked, speaking very quietly.
'They left about half an hour ago, monsieur.'
'Half an hour? So suddenly?'
'There was a telephone call from Master Robert, monsieur, and they left in minutes.'
'Robert telephoned,' Wilde said. 'Half an hour ago.'
While he had been accommodating Françoise in the long
grass. Oh, he had his troubles, all right; Lucinda hadn't
been wrong about that.
'Monsieur?' Aimee inquired, anxiously.
'I'm sorry, mademoiselle. It is no business of mine.' Wilde
went past her, hurried towards his room. Now the bell had
stopped ringing; so now he must start thinking, very quickly,
very clearly, and very accurately. Robert had telephoned from
the village, moments after he had sent Wilde and his sister
back to the château. Saying? There is a copper down here;
get Madeleine out of the house? But there had not been
time for him to make sure the stranger was a detective.
So perhaps he had been sure from the start. So why Madeleine? Because they *knew* she had written a letter; at least one
to the Sûreté? Hardly likely; according to Lucinda, one of
these men was a cold-blooded killer, and Madeleine was no
blood relative. Because they knew that a letter had been written, but not the name of the writer? That made more sense.
Only this afternoon Madeleine had been found in the room
of Jules Romain, one of the two strangers who so unusually
had come to Dort in December. Madeleine had to be inter-
rogated. But not in Dort, where the two strangers were already in residence. So they had sent her to Paris. But not

they. Only Jack. The tense one. The one with the strong, nervous fingers. The O'Dowd with the most reason for avoiding an inquisitive detective. An O'Dowd who had been away last week. It all fell rather neatly into place.

But with his mother, as chaperone?

He entered his bedroom, picked up the keys to the hire car, threw them into the air, caught them again. What good were they to him, now? There were several routes to Paris. And then the whole city. *They* would know where Madeleine was going. But they were unlikely to confide in Jules Romain. He frowned at himself in the mirror; there was a trace of lipstick on his collar. Not *they*. So she was an anxious innocent, almost halfway round the bend with frustration, and with fear as well, he thought. She could *feel* there was something wrong with her brother. With all of her family, perhaps. So with it all, she was a nice girl, who trusted him. He was Jonas Wilde, and he had been sent here to do a job of work. Niceness, trustworthiness, did not come into it. Only Lucinda, and Gerald Light, mattered now. Only by believing that had he stayed alive for forty years.

He opened the door, faced Maurice O'Dowd. 'Jules!' Maurice said. 'I thought I heard your voice, talking with Aimee, was it? But you cannot mope in your bedroom. Do you play billiards? Then let us have a game.'

His eyes were flat, and his gaze flickered away from Wilde's, and over the room behind. So Robert had not only said, get Madeleine away; he had also said, keep Jules Romain occupied, until I get home. Until we can find out something more about him. Judging by what Françoise had told him, Robert must have suspected him from the beginning, hence the invitation to stay. Any stranger was unwelcome in Dort. Two were two too many.

But there was a point which perhaps had not occurred to Robert O'Dowd. Certainly it had not occurred to Lucinda, supposing as he had that there was only one O'Dowd, a respectable resident of the village of Dort. These brothers were closing their ranks to protect Jack; if that were the case they could no more resort to the law than could Wilde. The thought was instantaneous, his fist was already closed, and driving into Maurice O'Dowd's waist, exploding like a hand grenade. Maurice gave a gasp, and his head came forward. But he was tougher than he looked. He had seen the blow coming just in time to tense his stomach muscles, and he was far from out. His arms came up and round to grip Wilde's waist and force him backwards. His back, the back of his neck and his head, were unprotected. But Maurice O'Dowd was not his target. Wilde brought his hands together, and struck them downwards in a conventional blow. Maurice O'Dowd grunted, his hands slipped, and relaxed. Wilde seized his collar with his left hand, pulled him straight, closed his fist again, and hit him on the chin. Unable to ride the blow, Maurice O'Dowd uttered not a sound. His head moved backwards, and his whole body sagged. Gently Wilde lowered him to the floor, stepped over him, into the corridor. Françoise was just reaching the head of the stairs, still absently buttoning her cardigan.

She frowned at him, 'Jules? What is the matter?'

Wilde ran towards her. 'Come on.' He grasped her arm.

'Come on? Come on, where?'

'We're getting out of here. I'm getting out of here. Will you come with me?'

Her mouth was a round O of delight. 'You mean you wish me to run away? With you?'

'Yes.' He was already pushing her towards the stairs.

'But . . . just now . . .'

'I was playing hard to get. But your brother apparently saw us in the wood.'

'Oh, my God!' They reached the foot of the stairs, hurried for the front door. 'In the wood? But that is not possible. Why should he be in the wood?'

'Don't ask me, darling. But he was. He was just in my room, accusing me of raping you.'

'Oh, my God!' She waved her arm. 'Sssh, Ney! Sssh, Soult!' The two little dogs came bounding up to them again, both growling on this occasion. 'They really do not like you, Jules.' She clapped her hands, and the dogs retreated. Françoise pushed Wilde through the front door, closed it behind herself. In the five minutes they had been inside the breeze had risen still further. It scattered her hair like an auburn cloud, and she had to use both hands to clear her eyes. 'But what did you do?'

'I hit him.'

She checked at the head of the steps. 'You hit Maurice?'

Wilde showed her the drying blood on his knuckles. 'That's mine, not his. Are you coming?'

Her tongue circled her lips. She needed time to think, to decide whether she could possibly translate her dreams into reality, to estimate the cost. But there was no time. The front door crashed back on its hinges; Maurice stood there, still holding his chin in his left hand, his immaculate cravat half undone, his coat torn. In his right hand he held an automatic pistol. 'Françoise!' he shouted. 'Stand aside. Run, you stupid girl.'

Wilde smiled at him. They were making life very easy.

'Duck!' Françoise screamed, and herself dived for the steps, rolling over and over and coming to a sitting halt at the bottom. 'Ow! Oh, my God! Did he shoot?'

Wilde collected her, threw open the Mercedes door, thrust her in and sat beside her. The explosion of the pistol came from very far away, but the bullet crunched into the roof. By then the engine had already started, and the car was swinging on to the drive.

Françoise sat up, panting, turned on her knees to stare through the rear window. 'He shot at *me*,' she said wonderingly.

'I think he lost his temper.' They were already at the foot of the drive, and Wilde wrenched the wheel round to send the car on to the road in a long slide.

'Ooooh!' Françoise squealed. 'Where will we go?'

'Who knows,' Wilde said. 'First stop, Ostend, eh?'

'Belgium,' she whispered. 'But . . . we have no clothes.'

'I'll buy you all the clothes you need,' Wilde promised, and wondered when it would occur to her that she didn't have a passport, either. Dort loomed into sight, empty as usual, only the pension showing any lights in the gloom of the early dusk. But at the sound of the car, Pierre came to the door of the bar, gazed at them in amazement.

'Oh, my God,' Françoise said. 'But it will do no good. To run away. They will telephone the police, and have us stopped, and brought back.'

'I don't think they will,' Wilde said. 'It would cause too much of a scandal. I think they will probably come after us.'

'Oh.' She subsided on to the seat. 'What a strange day. And it is just before Christmas. Jules? Will you marry me, Jules?'

'Of course. Although I do not think we will have the time before we get to Ostend. But if you wish I will promise you that I will not touch you until you are married.'

'Oh, Jules, you are sweet.' She put her arms round his neck, kissed him on the cheek. The Mercedes slid to and fro across the road. The eternal flame of Pauillac was in sight. 'You are so serious. So good. I did not mean that. Of course we need not wait. I do not want to wait. But I want to marry you, too. I want to go home. We can only go home if we are married. Oh, perhaps you are afraid of my brothers. But they will do nothing, if Mama tells them not to. And Mama will like you, she will love you, when we are married.' She lay down on the seat, her head on his lap, smiled at him. 'My Christmas present,' she whispered. 'Oh, it is going to be a Christmas I will never forget.'

(ii)

It was dark by the time they crossed the bridge and took the N10 for Angoulême. By then Wilde had selected his tactics. Presumably it would be simple enough to find some deserted sideturning and knock what he wanted out of this girl, and then leave her body in a ditch. Simple, and utterly distasteful. Perhaps ten years ago, when the job was everything, and people existed only as tools, or impediments, he might have chosen that way. Now, as he was constantly being reminded, he was involved. Too involved. Death was his business, but death outside the strictest line of business was unthinkable. And he liked her. Just as he had liked Robert O'Dowd, instantaneously. He was lucky that neither was his target, that he had not had the time to grow to like Jack O'Dowd.

Besides, there was another, simpler approach. To Françoise O'Dowd, of the Château Dort. She was still wearing her riding gear, and her shirt was silk. It would mean, what? The utter destruction of her faith in human nature. But for a girl like Françoise that might be a blessing in disguise. And she was young, and resilient. And when he was done, she would still be alive, and healthy, and able to look for life, all over again. Given time.

She was sitting up now, gazing through the window. 'Cigarette?' Wilde asked.

'I do not smoke,' she said. 'But you do, please, if you wish, Jules.'

'Thanks.' He found a cigar, bit the end, used the dashboard lighter. The car hummed quietly, the speedometer hovered at the hundred kilometre mark, lights dashed by in either direction. 'This is a nice car.'

'It is a beauty. Robert will be so angry. But I'm sure we are all going to be friends again, provided you don't damage it. It's all that Maurice's fault, you know. He is so quick-tempered.'

'He certainly frightens me,' Wilde said. 'I won't feel safe again until we're home in Ostend, with the door locked. Have you ever been there, Françoise?'

'No,' she said. 'Tell me about it.'

'It is a beautiful city. You know, it sort of huddles around the docks, but what docks, it is really a vast esplanade, and you walk along there, we will walk along there, on a nice afternoon, and we will stop at all the stalls, and buy our shrimps, and crabs, and chipped fried potatoes, real English chips, only better than any they make in England, for our supper, and then we shall take the food back to the apartment, and . . .'

'Tell me about the apartment,' she begged. 'How many rooms has it?'

He glanced at her. 'Just the one, Françoise. You think I am a millionaire?'

'Oh, of course not. One room? But . . .'

'It's very convenient,' Wilde pointed out. 'The bed is a studio couch, you see. Not really a double, of course, but we won't mind a bit of a crush, eh?' He reached across to squeeze her hand. 'It is the cooking which is the real problem, because I have only the one gas ring. For boiling water, really, you see, but then as we can always go down to the front and buy ourselves supper, well, what's the bother. And the bathroom is very convenient for our flat, too. Oh, I chose that apartment with great care, you know, Françoise.'

'Convenient, for our flat?' she asked.

'Well, it's on the next floor, you see. Mind you, the people down there have four kids, and sometimes they spend hours in the tub. But the chap below that is a bachelor, and the two girls upstairs, well, we won't talk about them. They have a washbasin in their room. I suppose it's necessary.'

Françoise gazed through the windscreen at the ribbon of light leading them into the darkness. 'There is just the one bathroom? Between all of those people?'

'It works out very well, Françoise. But you see, well, the rents are high, and . . .'

'Is there a view, Jules? Tell me there's a view?'

'Well, if you have one of the front apartments,' Wilde said, 'there is a distant view of the Handeldokken.'

'But ours is a rear apartment,' Françoise said sadly.

'I will put my name down for one of the front ones,' Wilde promised. 'It will be necessary, in any event. They each have two rooms, you see, and by the time we get one, say in five years, well, we will need that other room, eh, sweet-heart?' He reached across and squeezed her hand.

She made no reply. Disconcertingly, though, she squeezed back. He realised there might be more of a generation gap than he had anticipated; it was at least possible that Françoise was one of those who thought it was sinful to live on the scale practised by her family. So what else was im-portant to young people? Togetherness.

'You want to have a large family, I hope,' he said. 'I mean, the children will be company for you, when I'm away.'

'Away?'

'Well, darling, I *am* a traveller. You don't want to forget that. I'm only home one day in the week, as a rule.'

Once again she made no reply. The time was ten minutes past seven, and the lights of Angoulême were ahead. Wilde stayed with the N10, for Poitiers and Tours. And eventu-ally, Paris. He figured they could make the city by eleven, if they did not stop for a meal. But by now it had become necessary to stop for a meal; she was going to be a difficult proposition. Besides, they needed petrol.

He glanced at her. 'Hungry?'

'Oh, yes,' she said. 'I'm starving. Running away is such an enervating business.'

'Well, then, we will stop for dinner. There is a place.' He pulled off the road into the glare of the lights from the petrol pumps, got out and stretched his legs. 'Fill her up, will you,' he told the old woman. 'And can we get a meal?'

She gazed at the Mercedes. 'Here, monsieur? There is a very good restaurant in Ruffec. Several, in fact.'

'Here,' Wilde insisted.

'Well, monsieur, there is a café . . .'

Françoise had also got out. She squeezed Wilde's arm.

'Let's go into Ruffec, darling. I feel like . . . like a steak, a five kilo steak, dripping with blood. And a bottle of Dort. Just to make me homesick.'

Wilde kissed her on the nose. 'Darling,' he said. 'I'm a

cosmetic salesman. I do wish you'd remember that.' He
urged her into the café, allowed her to hesitate in the doorway and take a long breath of the blue cigarette haze which
filled the room, smiled at the three truck drivers gathered
around the first table. 'Anyway, really, wine is a ridiculous
drink for people like us. Two beers.'

'Beer?' she cried. 'But . . .'

'You'll get used to it, darling,' he promised her. 'Beer is
good for you. It will make you fat. Why, look at you, such a
skinny little thing. We are going to fill you out. Ah, thank
you, madame,' he said, as the young woman from behind
the bar set the two beers on the table, and flicked ash from
her cigarette at the same time. 'Now, will you bring us the set
menu?'

'Couldn't we just have a look first?' Françoise begged.

'The set menu,' Wilde insisted. 'It is the cheapest. Next
thing you'll be wanting caviar.'

She held her glass in both hands, sipped, shuddered, gazed
at the three truck drivers. They were gazing at her. She
buttoned her cardigan, smiled at Wilde. 'Do you know, I
have never been inside a place like this, before? It is very
interesting.'

'I knew you'd like it,' Wilde said. 'I always eat in places
like this. The food is often surprisingly good.'

Disappointingly, it was. Lamb cutlets, potatoes and beans,
following a tomato salad, all extremely tasty. The young
woman flicked some more ash. She was not very tall, and
far too thin, with long brown hair on which the grease shim-
mered in the light. She also needed a shave. 'Coffee?' she
asked.

'Oh, yes,' Wilde said. 'And two more beers.'

Françoise had already finished her meal. Her head jerked,
and she peered into her glass once again, and then, with
great resolution, picked it up and drained it. The truck
drivers applauded. Françoise reached across the table to hold
Wilde's hand. 'I am sorry I have been so unreasonable,
Jules. Truly. Perhaps you took me too much by surprise,

rushing me away like that. But I will do better, my darling.
Could I have a cigarette?'

And he had thought he had a problem before. 'I'm afraid
I only have cigars.'

'Oh, then a cigar will do. It will last longer.'

"You bite the end,' he explained.

She did so, and made a face. 'I think I swallowed it.'
She blew smoke into the general haze, released his hand to
stir the coffee. 'You see, you are making me realise how
empty my life has been. How ridiculous, to drink expensive
wine, when one can drink beer. How absurd, to eat steak,
when lamb is just as nourishing. How criminal, to live in a
twenty-five room house, when one will do as well.' There
were tears in her eyes. 'And to think that if you had not
nearly been killed, we would never have met.'

Wilde finished his second beer. And how bloody ridiculous to drink beer in a crisis, when the only real answer was
a couple of quick cognacs.

'The bill.' The young woman stood next to him, her thigh
brushing his arm. Saturday was clearly her bath night, and
this was Wednesday; but she went in for a lot of perfume.
He estimated that she was not the sort of girl to be inhibited
by her wedding ring. And she was his very last hope. The
only way he was going to get Françoise angry enough to
ditch him would be to be truly nasty.

'I have been thinking,' he said, opening his wallet to allow
madame a long look at the notes inside. 'It is already nearly
eight, and there are several hours to go before we can hope
to reach the border. I think we should spend the night here,
Françoise, and go on in the morning.'

'Here?'

Wilde put his wallet back in his pocket, allowed his arm
to droop beside the table; it brushed madame's leg all the
way down. 'I am sure madame has a room for us.' His hand
came up again, out of sight of Françoise, stroking the back
of madame's stockinged leg, seeping under her skirt. 'Have
you a room, madame?' He reached the top of her stockings,

gently plucked the garter, moved higher. There was only warm round flesh, here.

She never changed expression. 'There is a room, monsieur.' But by now she was puzzled. 'One room.'

Wilde squeezed, very gently. 'You do not mind, Françoise?'

'Oh, no, Jules, but . . .'

One last squeeze, and Wilde released her, allowed his hand to reappear on the table. 'We will take your room, madame. And we will retire, now. If you will show my wife up, I will just go and park my car.'

The young woman moved a curtain, revealed a flight of stairs, waited. Françoise got up. 'Perhaps . . . we could drive a little farther, Jules? It is very early.'

'As we go farther north, darling, the hotels become more expensive.'

'Oh.' Her shoulders rose and fell. 'I never thought of that. Please don't be long, Jules.'

Wilde went outside, inhaled some clean air, moved the car from before the pumps, locked it up, found the bullet hole. It was not very conspicuous, right in the centre of the roof. He checked his watch. It was three minutes past eight. Actually, a stop here might just confuse the opposition. Jack O'Dowd would reach Paris by about ten, with Madeleine and his mother. Would Madeleine be under restraint? Almost certainly. So Jack would have things on his mind. But as soon as he arrived, there would be a telephone call from Dort, to keep him abreast of the situation. So, for a while, however tired he was, he would remain very alert indeed. Only for a while. Come two or three in the morning, and no sign of Jules Romain, he would have to sleep.

He went inside. The young woman leaned on the bar; she had unbuttoned the top of her blouse. Wilde leaned opposite her. 'A cognac, if you please. And have one yourself.'

She filled two glasses.

'My wife is in the room?'

She nodded.

'She is very young,' Wilde said.

She nodded.

'It is strange.' Wilde brushed his glass against hers. 'How men look for youth, for inexperience, and then find, pouf. You are busy here, madame?'

'Busy?' she demanded. 'In December? When those three leave, I will close up for the night.'

'Ah. Your husband?'

'He is a sailor, monsieur. He bought this place for his retirement. But that is a long time yet. His mother lives with us, but she is not well. I am left with all the work to do, myself.'

'You have children, madam?'

'There is a girl, monsieur. A little girl. She has gone to bed.'

'It is good,' Wilde said, 'for children to go to bed early.' He finished his cognac. 'What is your name?'

'Danielle, monsieur.'

'A pretty name, Danielle. Will you show me the way up?'

She came out from behind the bar, climbed the stairs in front of him. If it really came to the crunch, at least she had good legs, although they also could have been improved by acquaintance with a razor. She reached the upper landing, and they were out of sight of the men downstairs. Wilde leaned forward, slipped his hands up her thighs, under her skirt, and lifted her from the floor. She turned in his arms, slid down his body; her arms were round his neck. 'You are very strong, monsieur.'

'I am also very gentle, Danielle.'

She nodded. 'We are poor people.'

Wilde released her, took out his wallet, gave her a fifty-franc note. 'Another, later on.'

She gazed at it for a moment, then folded it into her palm. 'Strong, and hungry, monsieur.'

'Very hungry.' He took her face between his hands, kissed

her on the lips. 'I will listen.' He stepped past her, knocked once on the bedroom door.

'Is that you, Jules?' The door opened, Françoise peered at him, her face a pale shadow in the dim light. Then she stepped back. She wore her briefs, kept her arms folded across her chest. She shivered. 'This place is just terrible,' she said. 'It is so cold. And so unpleasant. I'm sure I heard a mouse.'

'Cockroaches, I should think.' He went to the window, parted the blind, looked down at the truck, closed the blind again.

'Jules,' she said.

He went back to her, took her in his arms, kissed her on the lips.

'Oh, Jules,' she whispered. 'Jules. I had anticipated so much, on the first night. Jules! Jules! But what does the place matter? It is the people. The man and the woman. Is that not so, Jules?'

'You get into bed,' he said. 'It will be warmer, there.'

She hesitated, slipped down her briefs, climbed beneath the blanket. Nymphs, he thought, always nymphs. But Danielle was no nymph. Danielle would be a tropical rain forest, not a well-tended lawn. If it came to the crunch.

He poured water from the cracked china ewer, rinsed his hands.

'We do not even have a toothbrush,' Françoise said. 'And you do not have a shaver.'

'We will stop in Ruffec tomorrow morning, and buy what we need.'

'And could I buy a dress?' She sat up, the blanket folded across her lap. 'I feel so stupid, driving across France in riding breeches. And a brush. Look at my hair. I give it two hundred strokes, each night, at home.'

'We'll have to see,' he said. 'Nothing expensive.'

She pouted. 'Money. Money. Always money.'

'It's a fact of life.' He undressed to his underpants. 'Roll over.'

'But, Jules . . .'

He sat on the bed, took her in his arms. 'Remember what
I said? We marry first.'

'Oh, Jules. Well, at least make love to me, just a little. It
will warm us up.'

He made love to her, quite a lot. She was an utterly de-
lightful child, eager, and anxious, and totally uninhibited.
She possessed a body made for a man's hands. Once again,
as in the car that afternoon, the temptation to do more was
tremendous; in the warmth of the bed it was very nearly
irresistible. And what did it matter, to her? This afternoon
he had supposed she was innocent. Now he could even argue
that it was a necessary part of his plan; what he was about
to do would be so much more effective were he to take her
first.

But he hated himself enough as it was. He had too many
more nights, to sleep alone, and stare at the wall, and remember what he was, every dreadful milestone in his life.
Françoise was a girl to make a man happy, but even more
than that, she was a girl to be made happy. Making
Françoise happy would insure happiness, because she appre-
ciated so much. But her name was Françoise O'Dowd, and
she had dreamed of a nightmare, coming to her home, and
had awakened screaming. Perhaps, in time, it *would* be all
just a nightmare, when she was happily married, and had
her children. Perhaps.

She had the confidence, the utter relaxation, of youth.
Within moments she was asleep, her head on his shoulder,
her arm across his stomach, her breasts inflating gently into
his armpit. Her red hair lay in a vast cloud over and under
the sheet. And downstairs a truck started up.

Wilde extracted his left arm from beneath the blanket,
looked at his watch. But it was hardly necessary. This was a
very old house, and every sound travelled. He listened to
the bang of the front door closing, the scraping of the bolt.
He listened to the stairs creaking, and then a board on the

landing, the soft click of the door next to theirs. He heard
the splash of water, and even the ping! of a bedspring. He
sat up, thrust his feet out of bed, allowed his elbow to travel
backwards and jolt François in the ribs.

'Eh?' She also sat up, shaking her head. 'Jules? What is
the matter?'

'Nothing is the matter. I am going to the toilet. Go back
to sleep.' He opened the bedroom door, stepped into the
corridor. He took a few steps, so that the floor would creak,
then checked, and studied his watch again. He waited five
full minutes, and then very gently opened Danielle's door.

The light was on, and she sat up in bed, naked, smoking
a cigarette. 'Your wife sleeps?'

'Oh, yes.' He crossed the room, reached for her. She had
small, overworked breasts. She was not his type. He was not
sure that she was really any man's type. But he had just got
out of Françoise's bed, and she could see that.

She smiled at him. 'Monsieur is still hungry,' she said, and
placed both hands on his chest. 'There was to be another fifty
francs.'

'I don't carry a wallet in my undies, sweetheart,' Wilde
said. 'Put it on the bill.'

'And then you will refuse to pay,' she said. 'I know you
travelling men. And you, with that little girl tucked away
next door, you are a pig, monsieur. I will have the money
now.'

'Like hell you will.' Wilde parted her arms, and in the
same instant heard the landing creak. 'You do not understand,' he said, raising his voice. 'Being with her, brrr, it gives
a man the creeps. She is frigid. She weeps, all the time, and
talks of her mother.'

The door opened. 'Jules?' Françoise's voice was hardly
more than a whisper.

Wilde turned. 'I told you to go back to sleep, Françoise.
I'm with a woman. Not a girl.'

'Jules!' she cried. 'Jules! I want to go home.'

(iii)

'For God's sake,' Wilde said. 'Stop being a silly little bitch and go back to bed.'

'I want to go home,' she said, suddenly speaking again quietly, gazing at Danielle. 'Now.' She turned. 'You can stay, if you wish. I will take the car.'

Danielle smiled at him.

'Bloody women,' Wilde grumbled, got up, and hurried behind her. 'Françoise . . .'

She was already pulling on her riding breeches. 'If you touch me, I will have you arrested for rape.'

'For Christ's sake, Françoise, you can't take the car and leave me here.'

'It would be what you deserve.' She was no longer shocked, only angry. And most remarkably composed. 'But you may come with me, if you hurry.'

Wilde grabbed his clothes. 'But, Françoise, back to Dort? You can't make me go back there, Françoise. Your brothers will kill me.'

'That also would be what you deserve,' she said. 'But I think they will only beat you up a little.'

'Françoise,' Wilde wailed. 'You cannot do this to me. Françoise, it was partly your fault. You wanted to run away.' He seized her hands. 'They will beat you, too.'

'It is what I deserve, too.' She freed her hands. 'I think I must have been mad. That . . . that whore. I don't see how you could want to.'

Wilde finished dressing. 'Listen,' he said. 'Let us be sensible, please, Françoise. Let us drive a little farther, and talk. You wanted to do that, remember?'

She went down the stairs. 'I wanted to do a lot of things.'

Danielle stood on the landing, wearing a dressing gown. 'There is your bill, monsieur.'

Wilde threw her another fifty-franc note, ran behind Françoise, helped her unbolt the front door. 'Françoise, be

reasonable. All right. So you are right about me. It would
not have worked, not if you are jealous. I cannot help liking
certain types of women. Perhaps it would not have worked,
in any circumstances. You want so much, I can give you so
little. But I did not harm you, Françoise. You know that.'

She had taken the keys from his pocket. Now she unlocked the car, got behind the wheel. Wilde hastily scrambled
in beside her. She did not look at him. 'So what do you want,
now?'

'Well, listen, you could drop me off in Paris. Then I can
catch a train for Brussels. That is not asking a great deal,
Françoise. We are almost halfway to Paris, already.'

'And what will I do, in Paris?' She started the engine. 'In
the middle of the night?'

'But you must have friends, or somewhere you can go?
Oh, come now, I'm sure your parents have a town apartment.'

'Robert has an apartment,' she said, half to herself. 'In
Auteuil.'

'You could go there. You have a key?'

'There is a concierge,' she said. 'Yes, I can go there. Perhaps it would be best. I can telephone Dort and tell them
that I am all right.'

'And their tempers will have cooled by the time they come
for you.'

She swung the car on to the road. 'And you can scuttle
away into the darkness. You are a creature, monsieur. A
creature.'

Wilde said nothing. The time was eighteen minutes to
eleven. He had three hours to wait.

(iv)

Françoise had made the journey before. She took the by-pass
around Chartres, picked up the N189 to avoid Versailles,
sent the Mercedes screaming through Orsay. Away to their

right a late flight whined into Orly. Françoise swung left again, through the Bois de Medon, crossed the river at Sèvres. They were already in Auteuil before she looked at him again. 'Where will you get out?'

'You go to your brother's apartment,' Wilde said. 'I will leave you there.'

She gunned the engine, slipped down a side street with screeching tyres, pulled into parking. She slammed the door. 'Well, goodbye.'

'At least let me walk you in,' he said. 'It is past one.'

She glanced up and down the deserted street; it was drizzling a mixture of rain and sleet, and was suddenly very cold. 'Very well,' she agreed, and walked briskly, Wilde at her elbow. She turned into a courtyard, checked again. Her hair was wet.

'I had better see you up,' he said. 'Just to be sure you get in.'

'If you wish.' She glanced at him. 'It will do you no good, now, you know, Jules.'

'I understand that,' he said.

She walked across the courtyard, climbed three steps, pressed a bell. And again. There was a shuffling sound from inside the door. 'Who is there? What do you want?'

'It is Françoise O'Dowd, madame. Will you let me in?'

'Mademoiselle Françoise?' There was a scraping of a chain, and the door swung inwards. 'But you are all wet, my child.' The concierge wore a hastily donned overcoat.

'I wish to change. And go to bed.' She turned to Wilde.

He had already checked the name plates; the O'Dowd apartment was on the second floor.

'I'll see you up,' he said. 'It's the least I can do.'

She hesitated, and then shrugged and went inside. 'You have the key, madame?'

'Oh, Monsieur Jack took that, mademoiselle. But I imagine he is still awake. He has not been here long.' She frowned. 'He is expecting you?'

'One of my brothers is here?' Françoise asked in alarm.

'Oh, yes, mademoiselle. Monsieur Jack, as I said. Did you not know? Madame O'Dowd is with him.'

'Mama?'

'Oh, yes, mademoiselle. And Mademoiselle Corot.'

'Oh.' Françoise gave a sigh of relief. 'That is better. You may stop worrying, Jules. Madeleine will be on my side. Now goodbye.'

'I said I'd see you up,' Wilde reminded her, seizing her elbow and urging her towards the steps.

'Would you please let me go,' she said. 'And you are a fool. If Jack and Mama are here, it is because they are trying to find me. They will not be pleased to see you.'

'I'm sure they won't,' Wilde said.

She tried to check, turning towards him. He had allowed his tone to change, and she had not heard that voice before. But now they were already past the first landing.

'Jules,' she said. 'You are hurting me.'

'Sorry, sweetheart,' he said, and thrust her at the door. 'Ring.'

She stared at him, her eyes wide.

'Ring,' he said again, tightening his grip on her arm.

She gave a little wince, pressed the bell. The door opened within seconds, and Jack O'Dowd gazed at them. Wilde's turn to sigh with relief. It could so easily have been Mrs. O'Dowd.

'Françoise!' Jack O'Dowd saw Wilde, and his face changed. He stepped backwards, tried to close the door. Wilde threw Françoise into his arms. She gave a strangled gasp, struck her brother on the chest, threw him off balance. Wilde kicked the door shut, reached forward with both hands, seized the girl, dragged her away, and threw her on the settee. Jack O'Dowd had fallen against a chair. Now he stood up, and at the same instant reached for his left armpit, thrusting his hand inside his jacket. Wilde grasped his shoulder with his left hand, spun him round. Jack O'Dowd struck the chair again, bent over, and straightened,

his right hand now free of his jacket, holding a Baby Browning. But for the split second, as he started to turn, his back
was to Wilde, and Wilde was already swinging, his feet an-
chored to the floor, all his fourteen stones of weight trans-
ferred from his thighs and through his shoulder into his right
arm, his right hand flat and rigid, and hard as a length of
steel piping. It crashed into the base of Jack O'Dowd's skull,
and he fell forward without a sound, hit the chair for the
third time, and this time he did not move again.

7

THE force of the blow carried Wilde onwards, spinning on
his own axis, for a moment facing Françoise. He reached
for her; the car keys were in her breeches pocket. She opened
her mouth to scream, but no sound came. Wilde put his
right hand on her chest to hold her flat, extracted the keys
with his left, straightened, turned for the door.

'Stop right there,' said a woman, in French.

He half turned his head, gazed at the second pistol, then
at Mrs. O'Dowd. She wore a dressing gown, and her hair
was loose. There was no softness in her face.

'I will kill you,' she said. 'If you move towards me.'

Wilde nodded. 'I believe you would.'

Françoise was sitting up, rubbing her head. 'I do not
understand,' she said. 'Jules? What is happening? You said
you were afraid of my brothers.'

'You could say I lost my head,' Wilde suggested. His brain
was galloping, but mainly in circles. For at least the second
time on this assignment, he had been careless. But then, he
had never been opposed to a woman old enough to be his
mother, had not supposed this woman could possibly be
dangerous, had only been afraid of having to hurt her in

reaching her son. But the operative word this time was mother.

'Mama?' François said. 'That gun. I do not understand . . .'

'There are a great many things you do not understand,' Mrs. O'Dowd said contemptuously. 'If you will wake up your brother, perhaps he will explain it to you. And you, Mr. Romain, please sit down.'

Wilde sat down.

'Now look after Jack,' Mrs. O'Dowd told her daughter. 'Throw some water on his face.'

'Oh. Oh, yes, Mama.' Françoise went into the bathroom.

'What have you done with Miss Corot?' Wilde asked.

'She is in the bedroom,' Mrs. O'Dowd said. 'Quite unharmed, at this moment.'

'And what do you intend to do with her? And with me?'

'That depends,' Mrs. O'Dowd said.

Françoise returned with a bowl of water and a towel. She placed these on the floor, held Jack O'Dowd's legs to try and turn him. 'He is so heavy,' she gasped. 'So . . .' She gazed at her brother. His legs struck the floor, his body slid down the chair as he half turned. His head drooped at almost a right angle to his shoulders. Françoise screamed, a thin wailing sound.

'Be quiet,' her mother snapped. 'What is the matter?'

'He's dead,' Françoise whispered. 'Dead,' she gasped. 'Dead!' she screamed. 'He's . . .'

'Be quiet!' Mrs. O'Dowd snapped again. But she never took her gaze away from Wilde, and she remained twenty feet away. 'Is my son dead, Mr. Romain?'

'I must have hit him too hard,' Wilde said. 'I'm sorry, madame.'

'You . . . you bastard!' Françoise shouted, and hurled herself at him, all tumbling arms and flailing nails. He caught her in mid air, already on his feet.

'Sit down,' Mrs. O'Dowd commanded. Never had Wilde heard a quiet voice contain so much anger. He had already

started across the room, but now he checked. He had been
in this business long enough to know when someone would
kill, and when they would not. He set Françoise on her feet.
    She struck at him again. 'You . . .'
    'Stop that,' Mrs. O'Dowd said. For just a moment her
gaze flickered towards the dead body of her son. 'You will
have time enough to work out your hate. If Mr. Romain
can kill with an accidental blow, the sooner we immobilise
him, the better.' She left the doorway, backed round the
wall, keeping always a distance of three seconds, counting
chairs and tables in the way, from Wilde. 'Now, go through
that doorway. Walk very slowly. Stay away from him,
Françoise.'
    Françoise stepped away. She still breathed heavily, and her
wet hair seemed to seethe. She stared at Wilde, and then
looked at her brother again, and dropped to her knees beside him. Wilde went to the inner door.
    'Come behind me, Françoise,' Mrs. O'Dowd said. 'It is
the door at the end of the corridor, Mr. Romain.'
    Wilde opened the door, went in. It was a large bedroom,
furnished in a pale wood, with the twin beds very low to
the floor. On the near bed Madeleine Corot lay on her back.
She wore a short brush nylon nightdress, in a pale pink. Her
arms were extended above her head, handcuffed together,
and then the handcuff was itself tied with a length of nylon
cord, which disappeared behind the bed, and reappeared at
the foot to link up with another pair of handcuffs securing
her ankles. She was awake. She stared at Wilde as if hypnotised, and then tried to twist her body away from him. As
an aid to modesty, it was a mistake.
    'You see what you so carelessly began, Madeleine?' Mrs.
O'Dowd said. 'You see, but you do not see. Lie on the other
bed, Mr. Romain.'
    'Good evening, Madeleine,' Wilde said. 'Or rather, good
morning.' He lay down. 'I'm sorry to barge in on you like
this.' But the situation was getting a little more serious than
he had anticipated. On the other hand, he did not relish

the prospect of taking two or three bullets in the gut, even if he could possibly reach the old lady at the end of it. He did not think that would accomplish anything worthwhile.

'Will you please straighten my nightdress,' Madeleine said, in a low voice.

Mrs. O'Dowd did so, with her left hand, never once taking her gaze from Wilde; it occurred to him that this rather gentle looking old woman might possibly prove to be one of the most dangerous females he had ever encountered. 'You will find two pairs of handcuffs in that drawer,' she told Françoise. 'And a length of nylon line. You will enjoy tying him up.'

'Until the police come,' Françoise said. 'Oh, yes. I will enjoy that.' She took Wilde's wrists together, and he listened to the click of the lock. He gazed at her face. She was holding back a grief which would very rapidly degenerate into hysteria. How soon? But the mother, so unnaturally calm, bothered him more.

Françoise secured his ankles, passed the nylon cord through each pair of handcuffs, and under the bed, brought it out the side and made it fast in a reef knot. She stood up, panting. 'Now, Mama, we can telephone the police.'

Mrs. O'Dowd laid the pistol on the dressing table. 'We will wait a while. Pour yourself a glass of cognac.'

'But . . .'

'Do as I say.' Mrs. O'Dowd stared at Madeleine. 'I suppose you are wondering what has happened. Well, Jack is dead.'

'Jack?' Madeleine whispered.

'Yes, my child. Jack. I am wondering if he did not have an illness of which I knew nothing. I have never heard of a man dying like that, from a single blow of the hand. But whether it was manslaughter on the part of Mr. Romain, or an accident, is it not what you wanted, Madeleine? What you started, with your foolish letter? This man, this apparently harmless cosmetic salesman, is an agent of the Sûreté. He persuaded this stupid little girl to bring him here, and when Jack attempted to stop him breaking in, he killed him.'

Madeleine Corot's head turned. 'You did that, monsieur? But why?'

'It was an accident,' Wilde said. 'He was drawing a pistol, and I got rattled.'

'An accident!' Françoise screamed, and once again threw herself at him. He closed his eyes just in time. Nails scraped down his cheeks, tore at his shirt, dug into his ribs. Closed fists flailed his cheeks and chin, crashed into his neck. Knees thrust into his belly and groin, made him gasp with pain. She got to her feet on the bed, staggering to and fro, and a boot crashed into his thigh. And now she was neither speaking nor screaming, just sobbing.

'Stop it,' Mrs. O'Dowd said. 'Stop it.' There was a crisp slap, and a gasp. Wilde opened his eyes. Françoise sat on the bed, panting for breath, and her mother stood in front of her with a glass of brandy. 'Drink this. You must not harm him. Not in any way that will show.'

'Not harm him?' Françoise whispered. 'Not harm him? But he killed Jack.'

'By accident,' Mrs. O'Dowd said contemptuously. She stood above Wilde. 'When I kill, monsieur, it is never by accident. Jack's brother will be here, very shortly. He may be able to teach you a thing or two about killing.'

Wilde sucked air into his lungs.

'Robert is coming, here?' Françoise whispered.

'Robert stays with your father. Like you, Papa does not understand. Maurice will be here, at any moment. He left Dort only an hour after you. Oh, he was not chasing you, Françoise. Not tonight. There are more important things in life than your virtue, you silly little girl.' Her left hand snaked out, her fingers thrust into her daughter's hair, forcing her head back. Françoise's eyes bulged. 'Without you, and without this idiot, nothing would have happened. Nothing would ever have gone wrong. Nothing *could* ever have gone wrong. She is the one you should wish to scratch, Françoise. But that poor creature is only a police spy who does not know

his own strength. Police spies have to be sucked up out of
their holes. *She* did that. Your friend, Madeleine.' She turned
her head. 'They have arrived.'

She left the room. Françoise stood up, gazed at Wilde.
'I do not understand,' she said sadly. 'I do not understand
anything. Except that Jack is dead. You are a filthy bastard.
You . . . you are an abomination.' She left the room.

Wilde sighed. 'I feel very badly about that girl, Madeleine.
I would like you to believe that.'

'Badly about her?' Madeleine whispered. 'She is a fool.
Totally uncaring about anything except her own emotions.
Do you not feel for us? These people are professional assassins, monsieur. And you have killed one of them. What do
you think will happen to us?'

'You started the ball rolling, darling. You must have some
ideas.' He watched the door open. Maurice O'Dowd came
in, his mother at his shoulder. Maurice's suit was as flawless
as ever, although his chin was discoloured. But his eyes were
more than just shallow, this morning. They were as flat as
if painted into place. 'Good morning to you,' Wilde said.

Maurice O'Dowd crossed the room, stood above the bed,
slapped Wilde across the face with so much force that his
head moved on the pillow.

'Do not mark him,' his mother said. 'What is your real
name, monsieur.'

'Jules Romain.'

'You are an agent of the Sûreté?'

'I am a cosmetic salesman, who happened to get mixed
up with your daughter. I apologise. I never touched her, in
any permanent way. Ask her. She must tell you the truth.
So I hit your son, and he died. I am sorry about that, too.
I cannot tell you how sorry, madame. As you said, I think he
must have had something the matter with him.'

'And this one?' Maurice asked, turning to Madeleine.
'What has she confessed?'

'She has said nothing,' Mrs. O'Dowd said. 'Nothing at
all.'

Madeleine Corot licked her lips. 'I do not know why you brought me here,' she said. 'You keep asking me about a letter. I wrote no letter. How could I? Am I not equally involved?'

Mrs. O'Dowd stood above her. 'You are a liar. We do not know what arrangements you may have made for your own future, what pressures may have been brought to bear upon you. But we know you wrote the letter. Or letters. Tell me about them, Madeleine. Tell me about those letters. All of them.'

'There were more than one?' Madeleine asked.

Once again Mrs. O'Dowd's hand moved with a speed remarkable in an elderly woman. Her fingers dug into Madeleine's hair, plucked her head from the bed, jerked her body upwards to the extent of her handcuffs, arched her slender frame away from the sheet, every muscle, every tendon drawn taut. 'Filth,' she said, and threw Madeleine's head away from her. The girl struck the bed, half rolled, gasped for breath. Mrs. O'Dowd pointed at her. 'You are going to die, Madeleine. You, and him. You are going to die. But before you die, you are going to tell me how many dogs are at my throat.' She left the room.

(ii)

'Nice old lady,' Wilde said. 'Makes me glad I'm an orphan.'

Maurice leaned against the chest of drawers, gazed at him. On the next bed Madeleine's breathing slowly returned to normal. 'Will you straighten my nightdress,' she begged.

Maurice did not move. 'Do you know what is the greatest sin of which a human being can be guilty? Innocence. Innocence leads to every possible crime. Innocence curdles the soul. The remarkable thing about you is that you are not in the least innocent. In any way. You only *wish* to be. Again. All over again. I am sure you are not embarrassing Mr. Romain, Madeleine. He has, after all, just finished se-

ducing Françoise. And she has a better figure than yours. Far
better.'

The door opened, and Mrs. O'Dowd came in. Her face
was inexpressibly sad. 'A quiverful. That is what Papa said,
once. A quiverful. And now I have two.'

'I would like the man, Mama,' Maurice said.

'We are not here to indulge our likes and dislikes,' Mrs.
O'Dowd said. 'I had Jack check the building when we
arrived. The flat above is empty. There is one woman on
the top floor.'

'And there is Madame Flaubert,' Maurice said.

'Madame Flaubert can walk out of the front door. There
must be no trace of anything that has happened here. Of
anything that has *really* happened. And it was Jack's wish
to be cremated. He will be pleased. If such a thing is possible. I do not know. I wish I knew.'

'But what about me?' Maurice asked. 'All of us, in fact.'

'Madame saw you come in?'

'I'm afraid so. And from what she said, she saw Françoise as well, and that man. Françoise is going to be a problem in any event.'

'I have given her a sedative.' Mrs. O'Dowd frowned.
'Madame Flaubert saw us arrive, too. So she knows there
are six people up here. And we have only three bodies, at
this moment.'

She was discussing a mass execution as if planning a dinner menu. Wilde glanced at Madeleine; stared at the
woman who might have been her mother-in-law as if
hypnotised. 'You are mad,' she whispered. 'Not just criminal.
Mad.'

'We have four bodies,' Maurice said. 'There is the woman
upstairs.'

'The police will know there was a woman upstairs,' his
mother said. 'And they will identify them by their teeth.'

'This is all a dream, anyway,' Maurice said. 'How can we
fake an accident, when one of the victims is a detective?'

'From the Sûreté?' Mrs. O'Dowd stood above Wilde,

pulled off one of his shoes. 'Kid. Made in London.' She
opened Wilde's jacket. 'No name. But it is an Italian cut.'
She took out his wallet and passport, flicked through them,
restored them to his pocket, pulled his head forward, looked
inside the collar of his shirt. 'Made in New York.' She let
Wilde's head fall back, jerked his tie. 'Silk. From the
Burlington Arcade. He is a much travelled detective. Perhaps he works for Interpol. But what does he earn? Perhaps
we have a commissioner of police in person.'

'I sell cosmetics all over Europe,' Wilde said. 'I told you
I had just returned from London. It pays a high rate of
commission.'

Mrs. O'Dowd turned to Madeleine. 'Listen to me,' she
said. 'It will save you having to continue lying. Last week
Pierre cleared the box in the village, as usual. He noticed a
letter addressed to the Sûreté in the mail, and told me about
it. The fool had not opened it, had already sent it on. He
was just gossiping. Who in Dort would be writing to the
Sûreté? So I must sit very still and hold my breath, and wonder myself, who? I must eliminate all the people who certainly would not have done anything like that, and come
down again, to whom? I must send Robert off to see Anton,
and explain the situation. I must wait, and watch. Then this
man appears. Accidentally? It could be. But Robert had
his suspicions from the start.

'And when another man appears our suspicions are con-
firmed. This second man has detective written all over him.
He is in the village now, asking questions. About Maurice,
and about Jack, and about Robert. Do my sons do a lot of
travelling? Where do they travel? When do they travel?
He is learning very little, because Pierre will not tell him.
Pierre thinks it is something to do with Income Tax, and
you know how Pierre feels about taxes. Tomorrow he will
get fed up and go home again, this detective. And yesterday
I knew who had posted the letter. I had suspected from the
beginning, but yesterday I knew, and I regretted having let
you live so long. I knew when Robert telephoned to say he

had seen you coming out of Romain's room. So we brought you to Paris. You were confused by the suddenness of that, eh, Madeleine? You kept asking us what we were doing, why we were doing it. You could not understand that you were being arrested. We were taking you to Anton. Anton would best know what to do with you. But when we reached the apartment Robert was on the telephone, about Romain, and Françoise. So we had to wait. Now we can wait no longer. But perhaps you are fortunate, Madeleine. Now, at least, you will not have to face Anton.' Still her voice was totally emotionless. When her grief exploded, it was going to be a terrifying experience.

Madeleine Corot stared at her. 'Mad,' she whispered. 'You are mad, Mama.'

'Let me work on the man,' Maurice said.

'You would be wasting your time,' his mother said. 'Whatever he is, he is a professional. Madeleine is not used to this side of the game. Are you, Madeleine?'

'You can prove nothing against me,' Madeleine said. 'You are making stupid suppositions.'

Maurice O'Dowd slapped her, even harder than he had slapped Wilde. Her head jerked, her whole body seemed to bounce off the bed. She gasped, and tears started from her eyes.

'Do not mark her,' Mrs. O'Dowd said. 'There is a probability that the bodies may not be entirely consumed.'

'Oh, yes,' Maurice said. 'I may not mark you, Madeleine. Except by fire. That will not matter.'

Madeleine opened her mouth to scream, and Maurice's fingers clamped on her throat. The sound died in a strangled gurgle. 'I will have a pear,' Maurice said.

Mrs. O'Dowd opened a drawer, took out a small wooden plug, shaped like a pear, consisting of two jaws connected by a spring. She stood above Madeleine, gripped the muscles at the base of her jaw. Madeleine's mouth opened, and Mrs. O'Dowd thrust the pear in, released the spring. Madeleine stared at them, her mouth held wide.

Maurice O'Dowd released her throat. 'No doubt you will
find some way of letting me know when you wish to
speak.'

He struck a match, plucked her nightdress away from her
body. 'This stuff really should not be sold. It is far too in-
flammable.'

Madeleine Corot stared at him, her eyes seeming to pop
from her head, clearly too terrified even to think. Wilde
could not see that either of them would gain anything from
indulging Maurice O'Dowd's sadistic streak. He no longer
had the slightest doubt about the quality of the opposition,
and Madeleine would in any event confess everything after
a few seconds of pain.

'There must have been two letters,' he said. 'One to the
United States Embassy in London, and one to the Sûreté.'

Mrs. O'Dowd's head turned, slowly.

'It was an American business, after all,' Wilde pointed
out. 'Still is, now I come to think about it.'

'Maurice O'Dowd's right hand flicked, and the match
went out. He left Madeleine's nightdress bunched on her
stomach. 'You are not an American.'

'I work for them.'

'What did the note say?'

'The man you want is named O'Dowd. You will find him
in Dort.'

'And they sent you to investigate. You said the man
O'Dowd. The note mentioned no one else?'

'The note mentioned no one else,' Wilde said. 'But we
knew there was a woman involved. Mrs. Walner was even
able to give a description, of sorts.'

Mrs. O'Dowd glanced at her son. Maurice O'Dowd
smiled. 'So you were sent to arrest Jack, and this woman.
Now tell me, Romain, if that is your real name, how were
you supposed to do that, in Dort?'

'I was not sent to arrest anyone,' Wilde said. 'I was sent
to investigate. We don't usually take much notice of anonymous letters. But this was a serious business. And when Jack,

and you, Mrs. O'Dowd, lit out with Madeleine, I knew I
was on to something.'

'So you tricked that stupid sister of mine into bringing
you here.'

'And then you killed my son,' Mrs. O'Dowd said.

'I lost my head, madame. When he tried to draw a gun
on me. I didn't mean to do him any harm.'

'So how would you say he died, Romain?'

'Search me. A heart attack?'

'A heart attack,' Mrs. O'Dowd said. 'It would be nice to
think that his death was inevitable. That it too cannot be
laid at my door.'

'Now, Mama,' Maurice O'Dowd said.

'Oh, do not fear, Maurice. So two of my sons are dead.
I will not cease to work for the other two. Jack died, perhaps in a fight with the American agent whose body will
also be found in the rubble. That is entirely reasonable.'

'Here now, hold on just a second,' Wilde said. 'I was going
to offer you a deal.'

Both the O'Dowds gazed at him.

'From what I've heard here tonight,' Wilde said, 'your
son Jack is the man we want all right. Now, I didn't mean
to kill him, but he's dead, which might just land us in
trouble with the French police. My boss would be perfectly
happy to let things lie, right there.'

'You take an over-simple view of life,' Mrs. O'Dowd said.
'And what about Madeleine? How many other letters do
you think she has written?'

'Tell her, Madeleine,' Wilde said. 'For God's sake, tell
her.'

Maurice O'Dowd released the pear. Madeleine's mouth
opened and shut several times. She shook her head.

'Of course you will deny it,' Mrs. O'Dowd said.

'I swear it,' she whispered. 'I wrote no letters. I felt there
was something wrong with Romain, from the start, so I
went into his room to search his suitcase, and he found me
there. That is all. I swear it.'

'I believe she is telling the truth,' Maurice said. 'And I think that Romain has a point. It is far to risky to kill them. Do you not think, Mama, that the Americans will suspect something must be wrong? They send a man to find Jack O'Dowd and a woman, and a couple of days later both Jack and this man are found burned to death, and the woman is not there? You do not think they will investigate further?'

'I think, in *those* circumstances, they very well might,' Mrs. O'Dowd said. 'But you have missed my point. They will find not only their agent, and Jack, but the woman as well. After which I am sure they will conclude that they have come to the end of the trail.'

(iii)

Madeleine stared at her. Slowly her head shook from side to side.

'There's an old saying,' Wilde remarked. 'About supping with the devil.'

'You are mad,' Madeleine whispered. 'Mad.'

'I am disappointed in you, Madeleine,' Mrs. O'Dowd said.

'And you are also stupid,' Madeleine whispered. 'Do you imagine that everyone else in the world is a fool? Do you not think madame will tell the police that you were here, with Maurice, and Françoise?'

'I am disappointed in you, doubly.' Mrs. O'Dowd sat on the bed. 'I thought that you would have accepted the possibility that for the good of the organisation it might one day be necessary for you to die. Now, shall I tell you how the Americans will see it, and the French police too? There is a murderer at large, by name of O'Dowd, who has a woman accomplice. This murderer killed several Americans in England; this seems clear because of the similarity in method. But always he disappears, immediately after the crime, and never is there any motive, any reason at all. And so the English

police are baffled. And then both the Sûreté and the American
Embassy receive letters, directing them to Dort. So they each
send an agent. The Sûreté send a conventional detective, because in their hearts they suspect the whole thing is a hoax,
and in any event, they are not too interested in who gets
murdered in England. The Americans send what must surely
be one of their lowest grade agents.'

'Unkind, unkind,' Wilde said. 'I'm very good with cyphers.'

Mrs. O'Dowd ignored him. 'Now, when they come back
to Dort, as they surely shall, it will be easy for me to piece
together what must have happened for them, although I
really know nothing about it. This American agent wormed
his way into our house, by faking a car accident, was invited to stay by the innocent members of our family, myself
included, and was then approached by the sender of the
note, Madeleine. Before they could talk for very long they
were interrupted, by Robert, who was to show Romain something of the wine industry. Robert and Romain went off
together, but Romain hurried back as soon as he could, to
continue his conversation with Madeleine. But Jack, the
guilty O'Dowd, had become suspicious, and so decided to
take Madeleine off to his Paris flat. He asked me to accompany him, as chaperone, and because Madeleine was not
feeling well, and I, being ignorant of what was happening,
agreed.'

'Would not Jack have dealt with Madeleine immediately?' Maurice asked.

'Not in Dort, surely. In any event, he would not yet have
made up his mind what to do with his treacherous accomplice. Now, while Romain is considering this, Maurice here
invites him to a game of billiards. Romain loses his head,
clearly a weakness of his, hits Maurice, I suspect he will still
have the bruise, rushes away with Françoise, whom he has
already seduced. His object is to persuade her to show him
our flat in Paris, and in this he succeeded. All this is per-

fectly true, as Françoise will swear. So they arrive here in
due course, and Romain persuades Jack to let him in.
Madame Flaubert will testify to their arrival, and he did
enter the flat. He is a most persuasive fellow, this Romain.

'But in the meanwhile, Maurice and Robert realise that
this man has run off with their sister, and they naturally
assume that his intention is rape, at the very least. Maurice
hurries behind them, cannot find them on the road, decides
to come on to Paris and continue his search here, using the
flat as a headquarters. He arrives here, discovers Romain,
to his surprise, and even more to his surprise, is not welcomed by Jack. It seems that his brother, and his friend,
Madeleine, have certain business dealings which they wish
to keep private from the rest of the family, and which in-
volve Mr. Romain. They wish to talk with him, alone. We
are requested to leave, myself included—Jack having no
doubt decided that as Romain has tracked him down, there
is no need to worry about Madeleine any more; they must
both try to reach some understanding with the man
Romain. So we leave. The three of us say goodbye to
Madame Flaubert, and drive back to Dort. We are puzzled,
offended, but that is all. Now, what happened in the flat
after we left is a complete mystery. The police will no doubt
reconstruct the crime. They will conclude that there was
some drinking, perhaps too much drinking, and then what
might have been a fight, which may have caused the death
of Jack O'Dowd, and also tragically, started a fire, a disastrous fire which consumed the entire flat, and, I suspect,
the entire building, and in which both Romain and the
woman Madeleine Corot perished. Oh, they will surely bring
this story back to us, and I will say, but, gentlemen, are you
trying to tell me that my son Jack was a professional assassin, working for some foreign government or organisation?
How horrible, and in the moment of my grief, too. But no
matter what they think, as the fire will have started *after*
we leave the flat, it cannot be related to us in any way.

Now, Madeleine, with your brilliant brain, tell me where I have gone wrong.'

'Do you think the police will not find the handcuffs?' Madeleine whispered.

'We will take the handcuffs with us, of course.'

'And you think we will just lie here, and burn?' she demanded. 'Oh, you plan to give us some more sedatives, of course. But suppose we are not entirely consumed, Mama? What then? There will be post-mortems. They will find the residue of your drugs in our intestines.'

'Your stomach, more likely,' Mrs. O'Dowd pointed out. 'But as you say, there will certainly be post-mortems. Bodies are very seldom totally consumed by fires. And the doctor will shake his head, and say, ah, people who drink, who drink to excess, and have fights, ah, what tragedies there are in this world. And he will be right.'

'You . . .' Madeleine strained against her handcuffs.

Wilde said nothing. He couldn't fault the old lady's ideas on what *should* happen. On the face of it, he thought he might just have got himself into the most difficult situation he had ever encountered. And after such an innocuous beginning, such an unplanned series of events. Beginning with his own preoccupation of yesterday morning, he had an uneasy feeling that he was still inside a skidding car, totally out of control, waiting for the crash.

There was only Mrs. O'Dowd's confidence, her contempt for the man Romain, her inability to conceive that the death of her son might not have been an accident, her total lack of knowledge of just who and what the man Romain was. But that had always been Wilde's greatest asset, the fact that nobody he had ever encountered, not even the professional assassins of the KGB, had ever quite realised they were in the presence of an even more deadly potential than themselves.

'Now come on,' Mrs. O'Dowd said. 'We must hurry.' She left the room, followed by Maurice.

'You,' Madeleine said. 'You lie there, dumb with fright,

or just plain dumbness. Don't you realise that woman means
to kill us? She is going to burn us alive.'

'Darling,' Wilde said. 'I do promise you that I'd do something about it, if I could. Anyway, she's promised that we'll
die happy.'

She turned her head, frowned at him. But she was too
afraid to think straight. 'It is all your fault. If you had not
come here . . .'

'I was brought here,' Wilde pointed out.

'By whom,' Madeleine said, half to herself. 'God, if I knew
that . . .'

And strangely, like Maurice, Wilde found himself believing her. Which left a great many intriguing questions to
be answered.

Mrs. O'Dowd returned from the sitting room, carrying
a tray full of bottles. Robert came behind her, with a second
laden tray. 'Now, what will it be? I have brandy, and Scotch
whisky, just one bottle of bourbon, some gin, and a bottle
of rum. There is some wine, too, but we will save that for the
end. I think we will begin with the brandy; it is the most
potent. Maurice, will you look after Madeleine?'

'You bastard,' Madeleine said. 'You . . .' She gasped for
breath as Maurice knelt on her stomach, and her mouth
sagged open. Brandy filled her mouth, and when she tried
to spit it back out, he poked her under the throat and made
her swallow instead. She choked, and retched, and by then
her mouth was full again.

Mrs. O'Dowd sat beside Wilde. 'Are you going to give
me trouble?"

'I hate violence, madame.' Wilde obligingly opened his
mouth. 'Courvoisier, is it?' he asked, when he got his breath
back. 'I'm not really a brandy drinker.'

'You are a very strange man,' Mrs. O'Dowd said,
thoughtfully. 'In every way. I should hate you. I do, but
not enough. But I hope you are just conscious when the
flames get to you, monsieur. I would like to think of you
screaming in agony. But, being an American, I suppose you

think this will not really happen. That it is all some kind of a joke.'

Wilde retched, without quite meaning to, and liquid spurted from his mouth and soaked his shirt front. All he had drunk seemed to have accumulated in his chest, and be only slowly penetrating his stomach. And now the bed had left the floor, and was floating. Dimly he heard Madeleine vomiting. But he had to think, very carefully, to calculate. He could not become incapable, too soon. Mrs. O'Dowd was no fool. On the other hand, if he left it too late, for all his years of experience as a drinker, and his considerable capacity, that would be that.

'Switch to the gin, now.' Mrs. O'Dowd's voice seemed very far away. And the gin made Wilde vomit as well. But before he could clear his system his mouth was full again. The bed whirled round and round, and the old lady seemed to be rushing to and fro. He gasped for breath.

'Now for the treat,' said a voice. Whose voice? Perhaps it was one of the bottles speaking. Oh, yes, it had to be a bottle. 'This is quite a good wine,' said the voice. 'Not a Château Dort, of course. Just a bourgeois growth. A good table wine.'

It was at least softer on his throat. He felt as if someone were drawing a razor up and down his tonsils. But now he had no feeling left at all. They must *expect* him to be out by now. His eyes drooped shut, and the room seemed to gather speed in its mad race round and round his head. Then there was a sudden excruciating pain from his genitals, forcing his eyes open again, as his body jerked.

Maurice O'Dowd was sitting on his other side. 'He can take a lot of liquor,' he said. 'Madeleine is quite out.'

'There are several bottles left.' Mrs. O'Dowd poured again. Wilde wanted to lick his lips, but he couldn't find his tongue. He realised that he had lost control of his bladder, but that merely seemed amusing.

'What are we going to do about Anton?' someone asked. The voice seemed to echo.

'You must go and see him,' said another voice. 'I will look after Françoise. You have your passport? You must tell Anton what has happened, that we must be omitted from their plans, for the future. Even for the new campaign. I have lost two sons. That is too much.'

Wine filled Wilde's throat, trickled into his system. His belly seemed lighter than the air which was already wafting him to and fro across the room. And now he could prepare himself. He gave a faint sigh, and his body sagged. He waited.

'He will not like it.' The fingers were back, driving into his groin like steel pincers, pulling and tearing and squeezing. He moved, slightly, but uttered no sound.

'He has no choice,' Mrs. O'Dowd said. 'I will explain what has happened to Robert. The man is finished.

Fingers plucked at his eyelids, pulled one open, let it drop again. The voices faded. Now there was a new problem, another overwhelming desire to vomit. But that would bring them back again. Even to breathe too deeply might be to alert them all over again. Hands moved over his, round his wrist, and his extended arms were permitted to relax. He listened to sounds, fought to control his bowels, to lie still. He heard a door bang, and then again. Time, there was the trouble. He wasn't sure what was happening, how long everything was taking *to* happen. He had no idea of how long he had been lying there. He had no idea how long it would take him to get up. But the effort must be made. He swung his legs off the bed, rolled behind them, sank to his knees and then to his face. It was the fault of the floor, which kept tilting this way and that.

He lay on the floor, and gazed at legs. Trouser-clad legs. He had moved too soon, and they had come back. Now he was done for. But these legs were extending from a seated position. Odd. No, not odd. They belonged to that fellow. He could not remember his name.

That fellow. He rolled on his back to have a better view, and smelt burning.

8

WILDE held on to the bed, pulled himself into a sitting
position. The room continued to swing round and round his
head, and he began to feel sick again. It took him several
seconds to focus on the man in the chair. But it was the other
fellow, all right. Whatever his name was. Jack. That was it.
Jack. The dead one.

Still holding on to the bed, he turned on his knees, and
promptly vomited. For a couple of seconds he was nowhere
at all, and then he was on his face on the floor, and the
whole laborious business had to be done all over again.
And always the nostril-tickling smell of scorching hung in
the air.

He regained his knees, rested his head on the bed, panting.
He threw his hands over the top, found a pair of thighs.
They moved, restlessly, under his touch. He worked his
tongue about. 'Hey,' he said. 'Lisshen. You. Whatever your
name ish. Mad . . . Mad . . . Madeleine. Up, girl, up.' He
dragged himself upwards, tried to stand, fell across the bed
and across the woman. A hand pushed at him, relaxed.
'Jusht take me to a brewery,' Wilde chanted. 'And leave me
there to die. Ooops.' He tried to sit up again, fell forward
again, discovered his mouth next to her ear. She had nice
ears, small like the rest of her. It took him a bit of fumbling,
but he got the lobe into his mouth, closed his teeth.

'Aaaagh!' she screamed, sat up, and fell out of bed.

'Sssssh!' he said, rolling across the bed, and falling on top
of her once again. 'Sssssh. You'll wake the neighbours. Sssssh.'

She lay on her face, gulping. But she was awake. Wilde
held on to the chest of drawers, stood up. The floor promptly
tilted, and his feet started to slide from under him. He got

them back, pushed himself straight, measured the distance
to the door, and ran at it. It took a long time coming within
reach, and by then he was back on his knees. Behind him
he heard Madeleine vomiting.

He wrapped both hands round the handle, got it turned.
But the damned thing opened inwards. There was a nuisance. Why did they build houses so inconveniently? He
kicked it aside, held on to the wall, got up, staggered into
the corridor, tried to focus. There was a thin line of ash,
scorching the centre of the carpet, running past the bedroom door, disappearing under the door to the bathroom.
Ash. A burned fuse. But already burned. A fuse leading
where? He tapped the radiator beside him. Gas heating.
Gas piping, somewhere. Surfacing, somewhere. Somewhere
which might leak. A bathroom was a logical place for there
to be a gas leak.

He staggered forward, turned the handle, and was thrown
backwards by the blast of heat and flame and smoke which
roared at him. A few minutes longer, he estimated, and the
entire flat would have been blazing anyway, so much pres-
sure had been built up in there. And at the side of the bathroom, on the far wall, there was a laundry chute. No doubt
going the full height of the building and down into the
basement, creating a permanent draught; the sliding door
to the chute was open, and the flames were already sucking
in.

He seemed to have been standing there for all eternity,
but it could not have been more than half a second, because
the flames were only now licking at his feet, consuming the
carpet as if it were soaked in petrol.

He turned, hurled himself at the bedroom door, fell inside. Madeleine was on her knees, shaking her head from
side to side, sucking great gulps of air into her lungs. Wilde
fell at her, thrust a hand into each of her armpits, set her
on her feet. 'Let me go,' she shouted. 'Get off, you great
beasht.'

He swung her round, pushed her at the door. She took

four steps and fell over, half into the corridor. That was sufficient. 'Aaagh!' she screamed. 'Aaagh!'

'Ssssh,' Wilde begged. He was immediately behind her, scooping her from the floor and thrusting her along the corridor and into the sitting room. The flames and the heat surged at them. When Wilde looked over his shoulder, the bedroom door was already invisible. And yet everything still seemed to be happening in slow motion.

Madeleine had fallen on to the settee. Now she sat up again, stared at the smoke. 'Aaaagh!' she screamed.

'Clothes,' Wilde said. 'Where are your clothes?'

She pointed at the flames. 'In the bedroom.'

'Coat.' He grabbed a fur-trimmed maxicoat from the stand by the door. Underneath were a pair of black boots. 'Thank the Lord for modern fashion.' He opened the front door of the flat, threw the clothes into the hall. The flames seemed to give a roar of delight, and made for the next open space. Wilde collected Madeleine, threw her outside, slammed the door shut behind him. The flames crept underneath.

'Put those on,' he shouted. 'And get downshtairs. Lisshen. Wait for me.'

Her head came up, and she tried to focus. 'You musht be joking.'

He held her face between his hands. 'Lisshen. They tried to kill you, too, remember? I don't want you. Without me, you're dead.'

She gazed at him, her head flopping up and down, her brandy-laden breath enveloping his head.

'Now hurry,' he shouted, and turned for the stairs leading up.

'You are a fool, Romain,' she shouted. 'You will be killed.'

Wilde slipped, and landed on his hands and knees. He kept on going, checked on the landing. They had said, no one on the floor above. He reached for the stairs again, panting, struggled up to the next landing, pressed the bell. No reply. He pressed again and again, cursed and banged. He

could hear the roaring of the flames from beneath him, and
the heat was back. Desperately he turned the handle, found
it was open.

He began to laugh, fell inside, closed the door behind him,
switched on the lights. The electricity had gone. He staggered across the living room, reasoned that the design of
each flat would be the same, stumbled into the corridor,
turned the bedroom door handle. He held on to the wall,
staring into darkness, willing himself to see. In the near
bed, someone sighed, and turned over.

Wilde sat beside her, held her shoulders, lifted her up.
'Lisshen,' he said.

'Why, George, darling,' she said. 'What a pleasant surprise.' She sniffed. 'You are drunk, monsieur. That is no
compliment to a lady.'

'Lisshen,' Wilde said patiently. 'We musht get out of here.
Fire.'

'Fire?' She did not seem alarmed. Her hand reached past
him to switch on the bedside light. 'No lights? There is a
flash in the drawer, monsieur.'

He scrabbled it open, switched on the light, gazed at her.
She had a long face, with high cheekbones and a big chin;
he suspected there must be a bit of Slav around somewhere.
Her hair was of an indeterminate colour, more brown than
black, he decided, and lay in a cloud on her shoulders. She
wore pale green short pyjamas, and was a big woman, with
wide shoulders and strong arms. She had truly enormous
breasts, surging masses of tiny blue veins beneath the pale
skin, wide, presently quiescent nipples; he estimated a bust
measurement of well over forty, and remarkably, there was
very little sag.

'May I have my turn now?' she asked.

'Oh, pardon me.' He gave her the flashlight. 'As you shay,
darling. I'm drunk. Not intentionally. Not intentionally, at
all. But thish fire . . .'

'Not George,' she remarked. 'Not George.' She reached
out to stroke the stubble on his chin. 'You have been drinking for days. It is a shame. That you are drunk, monsieur.

And that there is a fire. Or I would invite you to stay. You
think I should get up?'

'It'sh an idea.'

'Then hold the light for me.' She gave him back the flash,
got out of bed. The rest of her matched her shoulders, and
her breasts. She had quite magnificent legs, long and powerful. She pulled a dressing gown from the other bed, but did
not put it on. She draped it across her shoulders, walked to
the door.

'I wouldn't do that,' Wilde said.

She had already done it. 'My God!' she said, as a wall
of hungry red, topped by a rolling black cloud, surged at her.
Hurriedly she slammed the door, tied her dressing gown.
'There is a fire escape.'

Wilde opened the bedroom window, looked out. The
escape was immediately beneath him. And beneath that,
the night had come to life; great flames were leaping from
the windows of the O'Dowd flat, enveloping the escape itself, and the smoke billowed over the house next door. The
street was already crowded with overcoat-clad people,
shouting and pointing, gendarmes attempting to keep order.
In the distance he heard the clanging of alarm bells as
engines made their way towards the doomed house. Incon-
gruously, over everything the drizzle continued to settle
coldly.

The woman was at his shoulder. 'Brr. Wait. I will get a
coat.'

'Not too long,' Wilde begged. 'Not too long.'

He climbed through the window, held on to the rail. The
sudden cold air would be good for him in a matter of
seconds, he figured. And hoped. Right now it sent the world
tumbling up and down again, and the ground was a long
way away. Down there someone saw him, shouted and pointed,
and people began to flood towards the alleyway where the
escape ended. But they were pointing at the second floor
windows, as well.

The woman climbed out beside him; she wore a full-
length mink, although, amazingly, her feet were still bare.

Maybe she'd forgotten. But he wasn't sending her back; through the bedroom he could see the living room glowing. 'Come on.' He started down, with her at his elbow. And then she checked. Twelve feet beneath them, the escape disappeared in a cloud of red-tinged smoke.

'We cannot get through there, monsieur,' she said. 'We will have to jump.'

'That'sh concrete,' he pointed out. 'And to me a broken leg counts the same as a broken neck. Will you trust me, mademoiselle?"

She gazed at him. Now they were both illuminated by the flames which had reached the windows above them. 'Yes, monsieur,' she said, 'I think I do.'

'Then hold your breath.' He ducked, drove his shoulder into her groin, swung her from the narrow catwalk, his right arm locked between her thighs and over her right leg, her arms in turn locked around his waist, upside down. 'Don't let go,' he bawled, and dived into the smoke, feet slithering on the iron rungs. From beneath him there was a long ooooh! of mingled horror and fear, and then all sounds were lost as his breath was torn from his nostrils by a blast of heat. He choked, and thought that for a moment he actually lost consciousness. The iron hand rail became too hot to hold, and he let go and lost his footing at the same instant. He dropped perhaps six feet, and landed on another catwalk. The woman climbed off his shoulders. 'Come on, monsieur,' she said. 'You have done it.' She was below him, pulling at his leg. He turned round, sat down, and went on slipping from rung to rung. From above him there came a crash, and he was deluged in burning splinters. 'Hurry, monsieur,' she insisted.

He found ground beneath his feet, and an army of hands were seizing his arms and shoulders, dragging him upright. 'Monsieur? Monsieur?' A gendarme, peering at him. 'Over here, monsieur; the roof will be down at any moment.'

'There was another woman,' Wilde said. 'Upstairs.'

'Over here, monsieur.' He was led across the street. The first fire engine had arrived, was pouring water into the

apartment block, but there was no question of saving it,
now. Madeleine sat against a low wall on the far side of the
street, head hanging, still panting. A little farther down the
street Madame Flaubert was waving her arms and shouting
at a gendarme. 'You will stay here,' the first policeman said
to Wilde. 'And you, mademoiselle. There will be questions.'
He hurried off.

Wilde knelt beside Madeleine, slapped her lightly on the
cheek. 'Wake up, darling. The night is just beginning.'

'Your wife?' the dark woman asked, sadly.

'We're just good enemies,' Wilde said.

'You are an interesting man, monsieur. You made an interesting remark, just now, on the ladder. And now you are
no longer drunk. Do you really want to anwer questions?'

Wilde raised his head. 'Would you do me a favour?'

She smiled at him. 'Monsieur, I would do anything you
wish of me. Without you, I would be dead.'

'Then, will you go over there, and faint?'

She gazed at him for a moment, frowning very faintly.
Then she glanced at Madeleine. 'And afterwards, monsieur?
One meets so very few interesting men, nowadays. And one's
life is rescued, so very seldom.'

Wilde shrugged. 'If you wish, mademoiselle.'

'I do wish, monsieur. When?'

Wilde calculated. Today was Thursday, unless he'd lost
track somewhere in between. And he still had an awful lot
to do. 'What about New Year's Day? It's a Sunday.'

She smiled. When she smiled, the severity of her features
relaxed, and she became very nearly beautiful. 'That is a
charming thought. There is a square at the end of the next
street, a quiet place, with a fountain. Shall we say noon, on
New Year's morning? *Au revoir, monsieur.*'

She walked away from him. She walked well, on top of
everything. She reached the centre of the street, bathed in
the heated glare from across the road, was checked by a
gendarme. She said something to him, half turned, and col-
lapsed like a pack of cards. People crowded round her from
every corner of the street, running out of the darkness,

shouting and gesticulating. For the moment, Wilde and Madeleine were ignored. He held her arm, pulled her to her feet.

'Hey,' she said. 'Where are we going?'

'For a walk,' Wilde said. 'A long walk.'

(ii)

He walked her five blocks, found a small bar, pushed her into a chair, and ordered two coffees. It was time to take stock. He looked reasonably all right except for some scorch marks on his clothes, and smoke stains on his face. Madeleine looked very good indeed; the maxicoat hid her lack of clothes, and she had laced her boots. There were traces of vomit around the corners of her lips, but he cleaned those off with his handkerchief.

'You have been to the fire?' inquired madame.

'Terrible,' Wilde said. 'Terrible. I was one of the first there. I tried to get into the building, but the flames drove me back. Terrible.'

She made a clucking sound with her tongue, and returned behind the bar. Wilde studied Madeleine. She was slumped in her chair, upright, but with her shoulders hunched. Her eyes were closed. But she was awake. Presumably, he could just get up and walk out of here, catch a train to Le Havre, and be in England for lunch. His job was finished. He felt no ill towards Mrs. O'Dowd and Maurice for trying to get rid of him, in the circumstances, and the fact that Jack O'Dowd had had a large and well organised family unit to back him up was entirely Lucinda's pigeon.

Except that there was even more. Circumstances had rather fallen into his lap. To depart, without at least having a chat with this girl, might be to throw away some very important information.

'Come on,' he said. 'Drink your coffee. It will make you feel better.'

Madeleine sipped, shuddered. She raised her head, stared

at him for a moment, looked down again. She drank some more coffee.

'Where do you live, usually?' he asked.

'Is it important?'

'I thought you might like to boil me an egg. We've a lot of talking to do.'

Her eyes came up again. 'We, monsieur?'

'Darling,' Wilde explained. 'Those friends of yours just tried to murder you. In a couple of hours' time they are going to discover that they didn't make it. I wonder what they're going to do then?'

'So I must run,' she said thoughtfully. 'Where?'

'You want to travel in the right direction,' Wilde said. 'While you were sozzling, Maurice and Mama were chatting about someone called Anton. Who were they talking about?'

Her gaze shrouded him.

'I think you have just got to get things straight,' Wilde pointed out. 'You are finished, done, as a charming accessory to murder. Your only hope is to help me, just as much as you helped Jack O'Dowd.'

'And what, then?' she asked.

'We'll see what can be done.'

'We? The Americans, you mean?'

'Could be.'

She finished her coffee. Her shock was beginning to wear off, and she was just about sober. She had a queen-sized hangover, but so did he. She was just starting to be frightened, to realise exactly what had happened to her, the isolation in which she now existed.

'You are right,' she said. 'I would like to have a bath. I have a place, on the left bank.'

'You live alone?'

'Yes, monsieur.'

'Then let's go.'

They found a taxi, crossed the river, delved into the back streets of Grenelle. They walked the last two blocks, through

decrepit alleys shrouded in the pre-dawn darkness. It was
very cold, although the drizzle had stopped. They opened a
squeaking door and climbed an uncarpeted flight of stairs,
up and up and up. They emerged into a single large room,
with a skylight, but no windows. Madeleine switched on the
lights, which consisted of a strip on each wall, high up. The
room was remarkably bare. There was a huge iron four-
poster in the left-hand corner, a curtained shower and toilet
cubicle in the right-hand corner. On the far side of the
room there was a studio couch, a table, and four straight
chairs; in the far corner there was a small gas stove, next
to a free-standing larder. The vast space in the centre of the
room was occupied by a large mound of clay, presently
shapeless, resting on a dustsheet. 'Well, well,' Wilde said.
'Artistic, too. I would've thought your avocation paid better
than this.'

'It is not where you live that matters, monsieur. It is how.
Would you mind turning your back.'

He was not really used to modest women, not in his business. But he knew she was unarmed. He listened to the
thump of her boots hitting the floor.

'Thank you,' she said. She wore a dressing gown. She was
a most surprising young woman. And she talked pleasantly
to children, and made cups of tea, while she waited to assist
at the execution of their fathers.

'What are you going to make?' Wilde asked.

'Sculpt,' she said. 'I was going to sculpt Robert.' She went
into the cubicle.

Wilde walked across the room, turned at the table. She
was a surprising young woman. Although the room was
reminiscent of any artist's studio in Paris, it was different to
any other he had ever been in, in two remarkable ways. It
was clean. So clean it was almost clinical. There was not a
speck of dust on the floors, only a trace of a cobweb on the
high ceiling, not a single dirty mark on any of the rather
tired cream paint. There was not even any grit on the
groundsheet.

And between the bed and the room, the wall was filled.
It began with a large bureau, which grew into a glass-fronted
cabinet, perhaps twelve feet long and some five high. Madeleine's treasure house. There were books; Lenin, Mao, Marx.
This did not surprise him. The glassware did. There were
glass ornaments, stags, alligators, nymphs, hunters, dogs, cats,
not terribly good stuff, but each clean and carefully arranged. The goblets were better. Four of them were crystal, strangely huddled amongst cheap glass cups and saucers.
It was a totally tasteless collection, evidence of a compulsive
urge to possess any object made of glass, but so clean, so
evidently arranged and polished with the most loving of
care.

On the top of the cabinet there was a framed photograph
of Che Guevara.

Wilde whistled through his teeth, opened the bureau. In
the top drawer there was a Baby Browning automatic. She
hadn't made any final decisions yet. He removed the magazine, dropped it into his pocket. On the other side of the
bed there was a wardrobe. He opened the door, found a
collection of surprisingly good clothes, mostly hers, he supposed, although there were also two coats and a man's topcoat, which he thought might come in handy; it was
roughly his size, and now he was in a good light he realised
his suit was looking decidedly the worse for wear.

Madeleine emerged from the shower, wearing her dressing gown, towelling her hair. 'God,' she said. 'Oh, God.'
She lay on her stomach across the bed.

Wilde found some instant coffee, boiled a kettle of water.
'Come on, darling. You promised me an egg.'

She pushed herself upwards, knelt on the bed, the cup in
both hands. 'Who are you, monsieur?'

'I thought you had that all spelled out.'

'And they sent you after Jack O'Dowd?'

'They sent me to find Kevin Walner's murderer.'

She smiled, thoughtfully. 'I was there, too. I drove the
car.'

'And made tea. And entertained the kids. I know.' He sat at the table, on the far side of the room. He had had a tiring night. 'My brief was Walner's killer, nobody else; we've other people looking for the employer. But they're interested in you, as well, of course. They might just bargain, a little, if you're co-operative.'

'I cannot afford to operate on the word "might," monsieur.'

'I think you'd better grab what you can, right this moment, mademoiselle.'

She put down her coffee cup, lay back on the bed, one knee up. 'Do you find me attractive, monsieur?'

'You're not giving me much chance to form an opinion either way, darling.'

'You Americans.' She sighed, got up, closed her dressing gown. 'In many ways, I am beautiful. Robert always thought so. And tonight his mother tried to kill me. Would you object if I got dressed?'

'I'd be rather grateful.'

She went to the bureau, opened the top drawer, turned with the pistol in her hand.

'Now, darling,' Wilde said. 'Don't be silly. You're in trouble enough, without having a corpse cluttering up your own apartment.'

'You could easily be a prowler, forcing his way in here.' She was half talking to herself.

'And what would happen next? I'm the only friend you have, right now.'

'If I killed you,' she said, still thinking aloud, 'and then telephoned Dort, Robert would have to take me back. If I killed, for him.'

'You need another drink,' Wilde said. 'Tell me about Anton, instead. Tell me all you know about this business.'

She sucked air into her lungs. How much did she so obviously want to lie down and think. 'Get out,' she said. 'Go away. Far away. And if you ever try to come back in here I *will* kill you, Mr. Romain.'

Wilde took the magazine from his pocket, dangled it between thumb and forefinger.

Slowly she lowered the pistol, looked at the butt. Her arm drooped to her side. Wilde pocketed the magazine again, walked across the room. He took the pistol from her fingers, pocketed that as well. She raised her head, gazed at him. Her mouth was just a little open. He realised that she *wanted* to be beaten, forced into something. Maybe she really was a masochist; maybe she was just confused, desperate, miserable.

He stepped away from her. 'You were going to tell me about Anton.'

She ran for the table. He caught her arm as she passed him, swung her round, and pushed. She skidded across the room, struck the wardrobe, and sat down. She panted for breath and her dressing gown had become unfastened. She did not bother to adjust it.

He turned away from her, walked round the bed, stood in front of the glass case.

Madeleine Corot sucked air into her lungs. 'What . . . what are you doing?'

'Waiting to hear about Anton.' He took the pistol from his pocket, reversed it, tapped the glass, lightly. At the second tap it cracked, at the third the entire pane dissolved, fell to the floor in splinters.

Madeleine scrambled to her feet. 'You . . .'

'Not me. Anton.' He took out a glass stag, fondled it, broke off its legs, one by one.

'Stop it!' she shouted, and ran at him again. He lobbed the ornament at her, and she caught it with desperate anxiety, fumbling the catch and hugging the shattered ornament to her body to stop it hitting the floor. 'Please,' she begged.

Wilde reached through the hole, took out one of the four crystal goblets.

'Please!' she shouted.

He sat on the bed, the goblet in his hands.

'Anton gives the orders.' She stood in front of him, her hands clasped, the stag's head peeping out from between her fingers. 'He tells them where to go, and when, who to kill. He gives the orders to Robert.'

'And Robert gave them to Jack. Quite a family business.'

She gazed at him, frowning. And suddenly the alarm bells were back, still faint, but increasing every moment.

'Who gives Anton *his* orders?'

'I don't know. I swear it, Mr. Romain.'

'Oh, come now.' He held the goblet up, dropped it, caught it.

Madeleine gave a little shriek. 'I swear it,' she cried.

'All right. Tell me how you became involved. Where did Anton find you?'

'Anton did not find me,' she gasped. 'I work for Robert. I have always worked for Robert. I am his mistress, monsieur. I was his mistress, up to last night. I arrange the passages, the transport. I arrange everything, when Robert tells me to. I just do what I am told.'

'You're Robert's mistress, but you were engaged to marry his older brother, and he sent you off to commit murder with his younger brother?'

Madeleine's face relaxed. She almost smiled. 'How little you know, monsieur. How very little.'

The alarm bells jangled in Wilde's brain. 'So educate me, darling.'

'They sent you for Kevin Walner's killer, Mr. Romain? Jack O'Dowd did not kill Kevin Walner. Maurice O'Dowd did it.' Now she did laugh. 'But Jack killed Harry Adamson. Not Michael Rhodes, though. Robert killed Michael Rhodes.' She threw her head back to give a peal of laughter. 'They are a family of murderers, monsieur. What will you do, kill them all as you killed Jack?'

9

WILDE got up, walked to the glass case, replaced the goblet. As if it had not been obvious, from the beginning. From his first meeting with the family. He had recognised their closeness, immediately understood that they would combine against him with utter determination. But nothing more. He had been preoccupied, and perhaps taken out of his stride by meeting Robert O'Dowd at the Bordeaux airport. But the possibility of the truth had not even suggested itself to Lucinda.

'Monsieur?' Madeleine asked.

'You were going to boil me an egg,' he said. 'Let's get on with it.'

She went to the stove. Wilde washed his face, leaving the curtain open so that he could keep an eye on her. The cold water made him feel slightly better. But his head continued to buzz, and not only with stale alcohol. He had no option; he had been employed to eliminate Kevin Walner's assassin. And unless he acted very quickly, that might well become impossible.

He tried to remember. What time had Mrs. O'Dowd and Maurice left the flat? Say, three o'clock. He glanced at his watch. It was just coming up to seven.

He switched on the bedside radio. Madeleine watched him, ladling instant coffee into two cups. They listened to the usual domestic and Middle Eastern problems. 'Following the fire in Auteuil early this morning,' said the announcer at last, 'in which an apartment building was destroyed, and in which it is feared that at least one man may have lost his life, the police are anxious to trace a man and a woman who escaped from the building, apparently in a state

of shock, and may have wandered off. The man is described
as tall and dark, wearing a dark suit but no coat. The woman
is short and blonde, wearing a full-length coat and boots.
Anyone with knowledge of either of these people is asked to
contact the police immediately.'

Wilde switched off. Mrs. O'Dowd and Françoise would
be halfway to Dort, certainly listening to the car radio. What
would they do? What *could* Mama, do, save regain Dort as
rapidly as possible, and tell her husband and Robert what
had happened. What then? There was an intriguing thought.
How would that monstrous old woman deal with a situation
which had suddenly got out of hand? How would Robert
react to it? Because he had no doubt, had had no doubt from
the beginning, that of all the brothers, Robert was potentially
the most dangerous.

But it was no problem of his. That could be left to Lucinda.
Was he glad? Or was the correct word relieved? Mama and
Robert. His target was Maurice. So what would Maurice do
when he heard that broadcast?

'Your egg is ready.' Madeleine had boiled one for herself
as well, and sat on the opposite side of the table.

Wilde discovered he was hungry. Danielle's restaurant
seemed an eternity in the past. Of all the O'Dowds, Maurice
was the one without an option, at this moment. Anton had to
be told what had happened. Mrs. O'Dowd had mentioned a
passport. If Anton was not in France, he would not even
know there had been a fire in Auteuil.

'This character Anton,' he said. 'Tell me about him.'

'I know nothing about him, monsieur.'

'Do you know where he can be found?'

Madeleine chewed, thoughtfully.

'Darling,' Wilde begged. 'Don't let's start that all over
again. I'm trying to get you off the hook.'

Madeleine drank coffee. 'Anton moves,' she said. 'All the
time.'

'You mean he has a boat?'

'A barge, monsieur. A boat would be conspicuous. Anton

operates a barge. To a never changing schedule. This is what
people expect, of a barge.'

'I'm beginning to get the message. So he's always in a
certain place at a certain time. Cute. So tell me where he
will be this morning. Where Maurice O'Dowd is going now.'

'This will count in my favour?'

'It should.'

She got up, moved restlessly about the room, stood for a
moment in front of her mound of clay, perhaps visualising
what it might look like, eventually. 'I should have to leave
Paris,' she said. 'France, in fact.'

'I should think that could be arranged.'

'Even Europe would no longer be safe,' she said.

'I'll introduce you to my boss,' Wilde suggested.

'Today is Thursday, December 22nd,' she said. 'Anton will
leave Rotterdam at noon.'

'You have a good memory.'

'I am trained to have a good memory, monsieur.'

'And he'll be going north?'

'East, for today, monsieur. He will spend tonight in
Gouda.'

'Noon,' Wilde said. 'That doesn't give us all that much
time. Get dressed.'

'There is no hurry, monsieur. If you go to the Sûreté, they
will be able to telephone the Dutch police.' Having made
up her mind where her future lay, she was certainly anxious
to help. 'The barge is called *Sprite*. Anton is a romantic.'

Wilde rummaged through her bureau, found a pair of
tights. She didn't seem to go in for much more. A red woollen
dress hung in the wardrobe; it would go well with a pair of
black boots he found in the corner. 'Put these on,' he said.
'You'll look super.'

'I will be here when you get back, monsieur. I have nowhere to go. And I would prefer not to be involved with the
Paris police.'

Wilde finished his coffee. 'I couldn't agree with you more,
darling. So I thought that *you* might like to take *me*, to meet
Anton.'

She gazed at him, her head slowly shaking from side to side. 'Oh, no, no, monsieur.'

'Listen, sweetheart, do you have any idea at all how many barges are likely to be leaving Rotterdam, around noon, going upstream? So maybe one of them will be called *Sprite*. The police won't be very pleased at having to spend the rest of their Christmas holiday hunting up and down the canal system.'

'Every barge is recorded when it enters the locks at Gouda, monsieur,' she said. 'The police will find it simple enough to locate the *Sprite*. And these are very dangerous people. I would have thought you'd know that, by now. It is a job for the police.'

Wilde held her shoulders, steered her to the cubicle. 'Just get dressed, angelface, and leave the thinking to me.'

She obeyed him, mechanically. Wilde tried the overcoat from the wardrobe; it was a surprisingly good fit. Robert's? Strange how the thought of the eldest O'Dowd haunted him. But why should it not be Peter's? There were still quite a few questions to be asked, and answered. 'We'll need your passport, as well.'

She sighed, from behind the curtain. 'You are going to try to arrest Maurice on your own? Mr. Romain, you are out of your mind. He knows that you are a policeman, now. He will have listened to the radio, and know that you are not dead. He knows that I am not dead, too, and so he will know there is a chance that you, or someone, may be following him. And out there, on the canals, it is possible for all manner of accidents to happen.'

Wilde used her shaver to restore some order to his chin. 'Don't I know it.'

'Anyway,' she said. 'We'll never get there. The police are looking for us. It said so on the radio.'

'So you'll wear a headscarf and dark glasses. With that description they wouldn't know me if I went along there now. Besides, they're only worried we may be wandering around in a state of shock. We're not wanted for any crimes, yet.'

Madeleine reappeared, sat on the bed to lace her boots. 'But I do not understand why you are doing it this way, monsieur. You are a policeman. Why do you wish to attempt this on your own? We would be far safer if we handed the whole thing over to the Sûreté and asked for their protection.'

'Ah,' Wilde said. 'But I am ambitious, you see, Madeleine. To be frank, my boss thinks I'm a bit of a nit. If I can clean this thing up on my own, it'll mean promotion.'

'And if you do not,' she said, 'we are both likely to be killed.' She stood in front of her mirror, absently brushed her hair. 'I am a mess.'

'And you've already started on at least your second life, sweetheart,' Wilde pointed out. 'So let's go.'

(ii)

They caught a taxi to the airport, obtained two seats on the morning flight to Amsterdam without difficulty; it was a dull, overcast day, much colder than yesterday, and there were few travellers. Madeleine moved like a zombie, asked Wilde to buy her a packet of cigarettes, smoked them one after the other. For the moment she was still suffering from shock, the shock of having been condemned to death by people she trusted, and the shock of no longer belonging to the vicious world she had adopted as her own. And if her head was anything like his, she was feeling physically ill, as well. So she was uncertain of anything, unsure of what came next, fighting for survival because it was a natural thing to do. For the moment, she *wanted* to be protected, and he was the only available protector, for the moment.

He bought champagne. He needed a lift. She thought that *she* had problems. Perhaps he had never before realised just how simple life was, how simple it could be. He had no illusions about himself, about what he was. Sir Gerald's contemptuous remark, that Wilde considered himself a soldier in the field, merely carrying out orders, was the absolute truth, because without such a sop to his conscience he would have gone mad with self-disgust years ago.

In the same way, he had always been secretly proud that his methods brought him face to face with his targets, at the moment of truth. No hiding in an upstairs window with a high-powered rifle. No surreptitious planting of explosives. Ultimately it was man against man, sometimes man against woman—he had never made the mistake of supposing that either sex was less dangerous than the other. But this absurd streak of boyish mock heroics was again, only a sop to his conscience.

He was a killer, a predatory beast, a ruthless creature of the jungle. A killer with all the odds on his side, as a rule. Other men selected his targets, despatched him into the blue. As a rule, they did not wish to know how he went about his business. Secrecy meant safety, for them as well as for him. *His* secret was his professional efficiency. He had been taught efficiency by his predecessors in this business, and he had surpassed them all, through sheer experience. He planned with meticulous care, selected his time and his place and his mood, used to the fullest his twin advantages of anonymity before the crime, of lack of apparent motive after the crime, to take him to his target and away again, unsuspected. He had survived.

He survived still. Remarkably. Because yesterday had been the day after Catherine, and Catherine had made all else irrelevant. Yesterday he had set out on a mission without a moment's thought, content that Lucinda, with true American efficiency, had even booked him in and then booked him back out again. Yesterday he had clutched at straws, wanted only to get it over with and escape back to the new world he had so recently discovered. And yesterday was the day he had needed every ounce of acumen he possessed.

It did very little good to reflect that even had he been at his most alert, he would still be in this position. Possibly in an even worse one; he had at least managed to scatter the opposition, instead of having to cope with them all in their

own home. It did no good to argue that he had been sent to
eliminate an assassin, and he had done that. Wilde had survived for so long, not just because of his efficiency as a murderer. In the ultimate, his survival depended upon his value
to Sir Gerald, and the mysterious mandarins who controlled
the British Security Services, to Lucinda, now, to the Western
Alliance. To the fact that he never failed.

So, in order to maintain that proud, ghastly record, he
must now chase another man, this time without that essential cloak of anonymity. His only remaining secret was that
he meant to kill. Maurice O'Dowd could not know that.
Neither did Madeleine Corot. But Maurice would not be
alone. Anton. Nor would Anton be alone. Barges generally
required at least two people to be properly handled. And this
was unplanned, unreconnoitred territory. This promised no
fade out into obscurity. This promised to be the end of the
line. How goddamned childish could you get? Every assignment had always promised to be the end of the line. What
was different about this one? Only that this time he wanted
to live. The suicidal impulse was gone. He wanted to live,
forever.

He glanced at Madeleine. She leaned forward, still smoking, staring out of her window at the heavy clouds banking
beneath the aircraft. 'How did it start?' he asked.

She seemed to awaken from a dream, sat back in her seat
and lit another cigarette. 'Their name is O'Dowd, monsieur.
They have fought the English for three hundred years.
Longer, in fact.'

'So have several million other Irishmen,' he pointed out.
'But not quite in this manner.'

'It is a tradition with O'Dowds, monsieur,' she said.
'These O'Dowds. They are soldiers. They have always been
soldiers. Soldiers who fought the British. There are British
families brought up to feel the same about the Germans.
There are Jewish families now being brought up to feel the
same way about the Arabs. And it is an effective way to
fight, monsieur.'

'Oh, I do agree. But you see, most people call it murder. Now, something must have sparked it off. Tell me about that.'

She shrugged. 'About five years ago, Mama had the idea of selling Château Dort in the east.'

'Mama?'

'Oh, yes, monsieur. You have met her. You know what she is like now. She has always dominated the family, made the decisions. She used to do most of the travelling, too, taking one of the boys with her every time. When she went east, she took Robert. He is her favourite.'

'East covers a lot of territory.'

'I do not know where they went, monsieur. I do not wish to know.'

'You're not interested in whom you're working for?'

'I work for Robert, monsieur. I always have. We had just fallen in love, then. I was content to work for him, and for the cause. I have always believed in the Marxist cause.'

'You're not French.'

'I am now, monsieur. I was born in Montreal. But I came to Paris to sculpt when I left school, and I have lived in Paris, ever since. Now I am naturalised. So, I have fought in the streets, monsieur. Unlike Robert, or any of his brothers. But I think he was influenced by me, and wanted to know more about these ideas, these people, I believed in. He made a joke of it, of course. He would say, these communists appear to be civilised people. Why should they not learn to drink a civilised wine? I do not know exactly what happened, on that first journey. But he and Mama went east four times in that same year. And all the while he was talking to his brothers. Talking to me.'

Robert, always Robert. The natural leader. And Mama. 'So why was Mama enthusiastic? She's not Irish.'

'There are certain French people who have little use for the Anglo-Saxons, either, monsieur. I should think that of all people, the Anglo-Saxon-Teutonic group have the most enemies. And Mama adopted the O'Dowd point of view even more thoroughly than the O'Dowds themselves. You know how this happens. There was more, obviously. I do not know what else happened. One of the trips was for a very long time; they were gone four months.'

'Which of the trips?'

'The fourth, monsieur.'

'And the last,' Wilde mused. 'Before they went into action. Where did Peter come into it?'

'He fell in love with me, too. I think, I thought, that all the brothers loved me a little.'

'And Robert allowed this?'

She glanced at him. 'The O'Dowds are not as other men, monsieur. This is their great strength. They are as one. They *were* as one, always. But Robert was always the leader, under Mama. His idea was that because they were brothers, and indivisible, they were an organisation in which betrayal would be impossible. But men need women. So if they all shared the same woman, there was another bond, another possible weakness eliminated.' She stared through the window. 'I was important in another way, because I lived in Paris. I was secretary to the group, booked their passages, arranged their itineraries. Robert conceived of two pairs of brothers, working together, hitting, and disappearing. He considered us a commando unit.'

'But you managed to get in on the act, too,' Wilde said. 'Why?'

Again the quick glance, the hurried movements as she extracted a cigarette from her handbag. 'The first job,' she said, 'was to be done by Robert and Peter. It was all arranged, tickets booked, over by plane, back by British Rail ferry to Dieppe, where a car would be waiting. Jack and Maurice were covering at Dort, putting through telephone calls in Robert's name, signing cheques to be paid into the banks on the day he was away, everything. Robert and Peter came to Paris, to collect the tickets I had for them. And then, when they got to my apartment, Peter was suddenly taken ill, and the whole scheme seemed to be collapsing about our ears.' She looked at him. 'You know something of our methods?'

'Something.'

'Then you will know that our assignments cannot be carried out by one person alone. To be carried out properly, each operation needs two people. And the flight was due to leave in an hour. I went instead. Do you know I was nervous, monsieur? I have never been so afraid. And then, I have never been so excited. It was easy. And so . . . so . . . I do not know the right word, monsieur. It affected my body. To meet a man, and talk with him, and know that you have the power of ending his life, that that power is to be used, in a short space of time, that every second is bringing him nearer the end . . . it made me want sex, very badly.' She looked away, and flicked ash. 'And Robert liked them to know. Robert was the best to be with. He would tell them, just what we were going to do, and watch them first be amused, at the idea, and then suspicious, and then afraid. But by then they had been injected, and it was too late. One man, a man called Adamson, had to be restrained. He tried to open the door. But most of them were just too shocked, or too afraid, to move. It showed in their faces.' She sighed. 'After it was over, Robert and I made love. It was a night crossing, you see, and we had a cabin. Oh, it was tremendous. It was like nothing I had ever experienced in my whole life before. And because I had been so good, and because I wanted to, from then on I went on every assignment. I was amused by that. It was always interesting, always exciting. It became a craving. Although the others were not so good as Robert. Both Maurice and Jack had the idea that letting the men know was dangerous, that it was better to pretend all through that this was going to be a kidnapping, in which if he behaved himself he would not get hurt. Maurice used to carry it to absurd lengths, always determined to make the victim as happy as possible. He would say, "A man must die happy, Madeleine". Do you know, he even used to invite them to kiss me, after the air was already in their veins?' Again the sigh. 'No one ever did. I thought Walner was going to. But he didn't. It would be an excitement, an *experience,* monsieur, to kiss a man about to die. At the *moment* of death.'

Perhaps making her talk had been a mistake. Some of the lifelessness had gone from her voice. He realised that these people were not, after all, in the least like him. That they found a definite pleasure, in their killing. That it filled a need, a stark, hate-filled need, somewhere deep in each of their libidoes. Had he even been like this? He did not think so. Once he had been happy to undertake his duties, because when you are young life is all black and white, and very little grey. But happy, never.

And now there could be no doubt that he was travelling with a human rattlesnake, only temporarily quiescent. He remembered Sir Gerald's little homily in the taxi. And he had been bored.

'And Peter?' he asked. 'What was his technique?'

'Peter,' she said contemptuously. 'He only ever did one job. And do you know, he was ill? He had to open the car door, and vomit on to the road. I knew then that that first time, when he had pretended to have been taken ill, he had only been afraid. Not of the action, I don't think, not even of being caught, but afraid of what he was doing, of the crime he was committing. Because he thought of it as a crime.'

'There are one or two square-headed people who might just see his point,' Wilde said, mildly.

Madeleine glanced at him. 'There is no such thing, as crime, monsieur. It is a word invented by men of power to protect that power. Life is now, and always has been, a survival of the fittest. But in the past twenty-five hundred years this fact has become increasingly obscured, and nowhere more than in Western Europe and North America. For all those hundreds of years man's nature has been dictated to by the entrenchment of the upper classes behind a barricade of wealth and position and opportunity, so that it took just about all of those centuries for people to grasp that such a system *could* be overthrown.

'Even more insidiously, for all those centuries we have been subjected to a constant propaganda barrage, perpetrated by writers and poets and dramatists, as well as politicians and rulers, and above all, by the various organised religions, all of whom, of course, have a vested interest in the sort of structured society in which *they* flourish. The myth has always been that we must aspire to *rise* in the world, to achieve what the established classes call ideals, which is merely a word for *their* opinions, that physical possessions can make a human being happy, that man is happiest when he is at rest, that love is a stronger, more rewarding emotion than hate, that goodness conveys some sort of mystical satisfaction. We all know in our hearts that these are basic untruths, but we have been brainwashed for so very long, that we feel guilty for knowing that. And so deeply are these myths embedded in the human subconscious that even successful physical revolutionaries, like those of France and Russia, have sought not to change the emphasis of life, to find reality, to end the myths and return the world to truth, and man to his basic needs, but only of using the revolution to achieve for themselves and their followers the positions of privilege they have set out to destroy. That is why every revolution has been a disastrous failure, why the world continues to sink into a morass of cliché and hypocrisy, of squandering our dwindling resources in preserving unwanted lives and unnecessary institutions.' She paused for breath.

'I feel sure, after all that, you have cultivated another thirst.' Wilde rang for two more quarter bottles of champagne. 'And your revolution won't make that mistake?'

'I do not have a revolution, monsieur. I am only a small cog in a much vaster movement. But I do not think it will be possible for anyone to go on subscribing to the old myths much longer.'

He thought of the pitiful little collection of glass *objets*

d'art. And yet she spoke with the utter conviction of the
true believer. 'So Peter was scrubbed,' he said.

'I had to report on him to Robert. That time with Peter
was the only occasion in my life I have been afraid of failure,
of being caught. I told Robert he could never send Peter
again. And Robert told Peter. Do you know, he was so much
in love with me that it did not seem to matter, then. I think
he loved me more, because we had killed together, because
I went on killing, without him. When I returned from an
assignment he was like a wild beast.' Faint pink spots filled
her cheeks. And yet she could discuss death as if it were
nothing more than an interesting job of work. 'But his failure
stayed in his mind, his system, made him ashamed of himself,
and afraid, for the family. He began to be careless, to drink
too much, and drive too fast. He began to be dangerous, for
all of us.'

'Sweetheart,' Wilde said. 'I hope you're not trying to tell
me that Ma O'Dowd executed her own son.'

'As you will know by now, monsieur,' she said, 'Mama is
not a woman who shirks any responsibility. Peter was no
longer fit to live, fit to be an O'Dowd.' She shrugged. 'It
was just a matter of adjusting the brakes. The car went into
the river. The Gironde can be a terrible weapon, monsieur;
it runs so very fast. In any event, he was drunk at the time.'

'I couldn't agree more. And that's when you started writing letters?'

Madeleine lit a fresh cigarette. 'I wrote no letters, Mr.
Romain. I am beginning to wonder if there *were* any letters,
or if this is not all some plot to get rid of me.'

'There was *a* letter, darling. And I suspect that if Mama
had just wanted to get rid of you, she'd have dumped you
in an acid bath and scrubbed your back herself. Where does
Pa O'Dowd fit into all this?'

'Old Charlie.' The contempt was back in her voice; he
thought that was her outstanding characteristic, the cold contempt in which she held all mankind. Her colour was a
Windsor grey, her personality no more distinct. 'Pa knows

nothing. Wine is his whole life, and the wine sells well. He has not left Dort in ten years.'

'And poor little Françoise is being steered in the same direction,' Wilde said thoughtfully. 'What *about* Walner's murder? Why was it handled differently to the others?'

She shrugged. 'Orders. I think maybe our technique had been *too* successful in the past. We were instructed to make ourselves more conspicuous. After all, we *knew* the English police had had no success in looking for us. The fact that the public would now also know these men had been murdered could not affect our security.'

'Only that letter, eh? I can't remember when I've spent a more interesting hour. Now what about the punch line. There are some odd little discrepancies in your story, you know. You tell me the O'Dowds are dedicated anti-British, yet they only kill Americans.'

'In Britain, monsieur. Only in Britain. Is that not sensible? If you are going to obtain maximum effect from an action, is it not obvious to calculate what *is* the maximum effect. So, Americans are dying in England. Is not an Englishman, and by a logical projection, are not all Englishmen, guilty? But we are only the spearhead of an army, a vast army. Do you not understand? We are the first, the prototypes, the storm troopers, fighting the first battles of the next war. We destroy Americans, in England. But the next organisation is already in being. Robert is himself to head it, during its first year. That will execute the English, in America. This confuses the opposition, monsieur, leaves the police, the real police, the *secret* police, not the ordinary detectives, unsure where their duties and responsibilities lie. Oh, it will be a long process. Robert estimates we may need ten years, but by then all the best brains in each country, and two or three others as well, will have been liquidated. And by then, too, every relationship that exists between the two countries will also have been destroyed. You will note that we do not destroy politicians. They are nonentities, transient figures. In point of fact, in the West, politicians change so regularly, and with them, their policies, they are positive allies of ours. No, the men we are interested in are the real strengths of a nation. And no one will know what is happening, until it is too late.'

'Would have known nothing, darling, but for that mysterious letter. So who *is* giving the orders?'

She looked up at the red warning light above their heads, extinuished her cigarette. 'I do not know that, monsieur. I do not wish to know that. That it is being done, that is sufficient.'

(iii)

Schiphol was cloudy, and there was still a trace of night frost on the roads. Wilde hired a Daf, took the road south, following the upper reaches of the Gouda Canal. It was nearly eleven. Madeleine was smoking again. He wondered how much of what she had told him was the truth. Remarkably, he believed most of it. She was too much the idealist, however great her contempt for the word, too much the real anarchist at heart, to have any desire to be mixed up in the direction and policymaking. She was a reincarnation of the women who had ruled Belsen and Aushwitz, who had sung along with the storm troopers, who had marched into battle beside the Russian legions. *It* was happening, and *it* made her happy. Sexy. That was enough.

Besides, there were other problems, now. She *had* managed to talk herself out of her hangover, her depression, her uncertainty. She was once again the cold machine who had reported Peter for weakness. So Mama had in turn decided that she must die for the good of the movement. Her sense of shock, of outrage, had ruined her composure, destroyed her own illusion of herself, made her little better than a female edition of Peter, for a while. As she had realised, while speaking. Now it was essential for her to regain her self-respect. Now, or some time over the next couple of hours, she was going to be an extremely dangerous young woman.

The road swung away from the canal at Leimuiden, just south of the placid Wasteinaer Plassen, and they raced between empty fields towards Alphen, and then Boskoop. They were not really very far from Rotterdam, but the roads remained slippery, and it was impossible to go flat out. Madeleine had sunk farther into her seat, so that she could not see out, arms folded, breathing smoke, thinking. Brooding. Planning?

And in Alphen there was a traffic jam. They waited in the centre of a long stream of cars and trucks, while the remains of an articulated lorry which had jack-knifed was cleared. Wilde sat still, both hands resting on the wheel, watched the monotonous sweep of the windscreen wipers; it had started to drizzle a mixture of sleet and rain. Madeleine sat up, stubbed out her cigarette. 'You are very calm, monsieur.' She looked at her watch. 'We will not make Rotterdam by noon. Not the docks.'

'You could be right,' he agreed, and let the car creep forward again. They crossed the Leiden Canal, turned right again, and now followed the Gouda Canal on its final stretch down to Boskoop. The brown water waited patiently beside the road; a single barge made its way towards Amsterdam. 'What does Anton do when the water freezes?'

'Like every other barge, monsieur, he does not move. Then the entire organisation takes a holiday. When the weather is bad, travel is not safe, anyway. There are too many delays. In our business, delay can be disastrous.' She hugged herself. 'Winter is a bad time for murder.'

'Summers can be pretty grotty, too.' He pulled in to a café just outside Boskoop. 'Come on. I'll buy you an early lunch.'

She sat opposite him, sipped a beer. But she was not hungry. Clearly, whatever she had in mind, she could risk nothing while they were in this most over-civilised, over-populated of all the Dutch states. But she was slowly tensing, slowly becoming excited. She watched him as a wife might watch her husband enjoying himself, knowing he suffered from a tendency to heart attacks. 'You have a healthy appetite, monsieur,' she remarked.

'It's going to be a long afternoon.' He finished his meal, drank his beer, sat back and lit a cigar. 'So you'd settle for a one-way ticket to America. I suppose that could be arranged, easily enough. You've never actually killed anyone. Have you?'

She lit a cigarette. Her hands had stopped shaking.

'Always an accessory. And presumably, as there must be some political motive involved in your assassinations, you could claim political asylum. Any idea on what part of the States you'd like best? Most people go for California, at least in theory. You know, endless sunshine. Except when it rains.'

She sat up, almost violently. 'Do you think you have but to say to Maurice, I want you, and he will follow, like a whipped dog? I do not even know how you are going to catch up with them, now.'

'Well, I'll tell you,' Wilde said. 'I don't run a barge, but in my spare time I sail the coasts, and the canals, of Western Europe. Birds of a feather, Anton and me. So I figure the Gouda locks are a better bet than Rotterdam. Come on.' He paid the bill, started the car. That had given her something to think about. Which was just as well.

About a mile north of Gouda, the canal divides, the left-hand fork going for the city itself, the right-hand for the main commercial locks into the River Ijssel. Some three miles north of the divide, the road is crossed by the E8 motorway from Utrecht, which bridges the canal before also dividing, one for Rotterdam, and the other for The Hague. Wilde joined the motorway for the bridge, then left it again, turned down a bumpy approach road which soon dwindled into a track. He switched off the engine, allowed the car to coast to a stop. Madeleine sat up with a start. 'What has happened?'

'Ssssh. Isn't it peaceful?'

The car was in the middle of a little copse of low trees, bare in the winter cold, but affording almost complete privacy. Behind them, the endless roar of the motorway traffic filled the afternoon. In front of them, a loud wail pronounced the arrival of the Amsterdam-Rotterdam express. To their left the lonely chug-chug-chug of a barge engine indicated that the canal was close, and to their right he thought he heard a cow mooing. The descending scale of civilisation. And in the centre, the destroyers of what was left.

'But where are we?' she demanded.

'A mile or so north of the Gouda locks. So we have to walk a while.' He checked his watch. It was one twenty-seven. 'I think it might be a good idea to start. It won't take him much more than two hours to come up from Rotterdam.' He opened his door, got out, buttoned his coat; it was definitely trying to snow, now.

'Monsieur.' She got out of the car and came round to him. 'I am afraid, monsieur.'

'Aren't we all?'

She gazed at him, her hands in the pockets of her coat. Snow settled lightly on her headscarf. 'You are a strange man, monsieur. When we first met, I thought, as Robert thought, that you were a man of no great intelligence, no great courage, no great ability. I thought perhaps your surviving all that alcohol, and getting me out of that building, was only a lucky chance. I thought . . . but no matter. Now, now I do not know what I think, monsieur.'

'Then give it up.'

'Yes,' she said. 'Yes. I shall give it up, monsieur.' She stood on tiptoe, her hands on his shoulders, kissed him on the mouth. Her arms slid round his neck, her body came against his. No puppy here, anxious to give. This was an exploratory kiss, lacking the excitement of passion for passion's sake, yet demanding, thrusting, breathless. And now he could hear her voice again, speaking quietly above the roar of the aircraft engines. 'He used to invite them to kiss me. No one ever did. I thought Walner was going to. But he didn't. It would be an *experience,* monsieur, to kiss a man about to die. At the *moment* of death.'

She was driving her weight downwards, pulling him over her as she leaned back against the car, and her right hand had left his neck. Not for the first time on this assignment he cursed his carelessness. And he couldn't afford just to kill her. He straightened his right hand, the fingers as rigid as if he was commencing his swing, drove them into her body just below her last rib. All the breath exploded from her lungs as she nearly split in two. The knife, already coming up from the inside of her right boot, where he assumed she kept it permanently—and he had selected the boots—sliced forward and opened a rent in his raincoat. There was a start of pain from his right leg, but it was an irritation, not the numbing agony of a crippled muscle.

Wilde swung his right hand. It was only a slap, but it carried so much power that Madeleine Corot seemed to fly away from him, turned a complete somersault, landed on her back, facing away from him. The knife had jerked from her hand, disappeared into the long grass. Wilde leaned against the car; his fingers rippled down the buttons of his coat, released the zip on his pants, let them drop to his knees. Now he discovered just how cold it was. The knife blade had sliced the flesh of his thigh, and the blood oozed out like fresh glue from between two recently joined pieces of wood. He had been lucky. He pulled his handkerchief from his pocket, tied it round the cut.

Madeleine was sitting up, rubbing her head. Slowly she turned to stare at him. Wilde dressed himself again. No one could see the slit in his pants beneath the coat, and if the coat itself was rather obviously torn, well, that wasn't a criminal offence.

Madeleine got to her knees, brushed some dirt from her shoulder, absently. And he needed her, still. So perhaps he hadn't been careless, after all. If this had to happen, far better now than a few minutes later. Only a few minutes. It was getting on for two. But she had to be persuaded. Permanently, this time.

Madeleine got to her feet. Wilde reached for her, seized the bodice of her coat, allowed his hands to drive on through the woollen dress and close on the small breasts beneath, dragged her forward, and thrust her against the car. Madeleine gasped for breath, and her jaw dropped as she stared at him. She expected the violence to increase. She *wanted* the violence to increase.

'Now you listen to me,' he said. 'Remember Jack O'Dowd? They couldn't figure out how he died, remember? So I'll tell you. His neck was broken. I did it, and I meant to do it. I'm not here to arrest anybody, Madeleine Corot. I'm here to kill. Killing is my business. Don't forget that. I'm here to destroy Kevin Walner's assassin. That is what I'm going to do in a few minutes from now, and you are going to help me, if you want to stay alive.'

He released her. Her knees gave way, and she slid down the side of the car to arrive in a squatting position on the grass, knees up, staring at him. Her tongue came out and licked her lips. 'Who are you, monsieur? You do not work for the Americans.'

'Do I sound like an American, sweetheart? Let's say, in going after Walner, your people bucked an organisation just as good as their own, and twice as deadly.' He reached for her again, held her under the armpits, set her on her feet.

'And you killed Jack, with a single blow?'

'Just the one.' He stepped away from her, took the pistol from his pocket, replaced the magazine. 'It's my business. Not hypodermic needles and pretty talk; hands and guns. If you so much as smile in the wrong direction, I'm going to put a bullet through your pelvic girdle. Right there.' He thrust the gun forward with startling speed, and before her hands could close protectively the barrel had driven into her groin. She gasped, and fell forward. He caught her, set her straight again. 'No matter what happens afterwards, Madeleine, you'll know what hit you. For the rest of your life.'

Her eyes were glazed. She had never encountered violence quite so primitive, quite so savage, before in her life. She was his once again. For a while.

'Now let's go.' He took her arm, and they squelched through the long grass. 'Talk. About Anton. How many people has he with him?'

'I don't know, monsieur. I don't know. Mr. Romain? Is your name Romain?'

'My name doesn't matter, darling.' They walked beneath the railway bridge, emerged on to the banks of the canal; the locks were a quarter of a mile on the left, the cluster of buildings and wooden piles stark against the cold grey sky. In front of them were six barges, tied to the mooring piles, waiting to enter. The lock was presently full, with barges coming up. And the water was very nearly at release level.

'Come on.' He gripped her arm, hurried her along the towpath, on to the concrete lip, jostled into the group of officials standing there. As Gouda was the southern end of the canal which started in Amsterdam, it was a toll station. But these barges had already paid their dues. Their engines were growling, the propellers getting ready to churn the dark water white. 'Pardon us,' Wilde said in English. 'My wife is fascinated by running water.' He pushed her farther along, leaned her on the iron rail. 'Are they here?'

She gazed from barge to barge, and several of the bargees stared back. She was a very pretty girl. 'No,' she said. 'No. We have missed them?'

'Unlikely. What about out there?'

On the river side of the lock, a fresh armada of barges was building up, nosing their ponderous ways alongside the huge wooden piles, mooring their two-inch diameter hawsers, swinging sideways with full thumps, coming to rest.

'Oh,' Madeleine gasped. 'Oh, my God. They are there, monsieur. On the other side.'

Wilde followed her gaze. The *Sprite* was not very large for a barge, and so she had moored by herself, a little behind her huge rivals. A woman with long black hair, wearing jeans and a heavy sweater, was securing the stern warp; he could not see the face of the man in the wheelhouse. A woman. Another woman. But it figured. Most bargees were crewed by their wives, and the *Sprite* was certainly a typical barge; there was a bicycle lying in front of the wheelhouse, and through the window of the living quarters he could see a bowl of flowers on the table.

He felt suddenly tired. There was no possibility of finesse, here. What was coming would have to be brutal, sudden, and probably disastrous. The gates were opening. It would take ten minutes to empty this lot, and at least half an hour to fill the lock from the canal side. The next batch of vessels from the river could not be called in under forty-five min-utes. 'Let's go,' he said, and half pushed her across the bridge.

'Oh, my God, monsieur,' she said. 'Oh, my God.'

Wilde watched a man leave the wheelhouse, clamber from the *Sprite* on to the towpath, where several other bargees were gathered, gossiping. 'Does Anton know you?'

She shook her head, and they kept on walking. The barg-ees came towards them, filed past them. Anton was last, a short, heavy man in a seaman's sweater. He never gave them a glance, pretended to be interested in the conversa-tion around him, but he was obviously preoccupied; if Maurice was on board, he'd have enough on his mind.

They reached the far bank. Wilde still held Madeleine's elbow with his left hand. His right hand was in his pocket, resting on the pistol. 'Bow your head,' he said.

She did so, and his arm went round her waist, pulling her close. 'Lovers, walking in the snow.' Because large flakes were now drifting softly downwards.

They stood above the *Sprite;* there was no one on deck,

now. Anton and his companions had disappeared into the toll-house. On the barge in front a man stood in the wheel-house, staring at Madeleine. Wilde gave him the two-finger sign and he grinned, and turned away. At the lock everyone was shouting orders, and all sound, even the rush of the river past the waiting hulls, was obscured by the roaring of the engines. Wilde stepped on board the *Sprite*, gave Madeleine's arm a tug, and she scattered behind him, her boots clattering on the iron deck. Wilde bundled her in front of him, up to the wheelhouse. He pulled the door open, thrust her inside, as Maurice O'Dowd hurried out of the living quarters behind the house.

Maurice's mouth fell open. 'Madeleine?' he gasped. His gaze flickered. 'Romain?'

Wilde shot him through the heart.

(iv)

Maurice O'Dowd made no sound, struck the deck with a thud. Blood seeped across the wheelhouse sole.

'Oh, God,' Madeleine gasped. 'Oh, God.' She dropped to her knees, fell against the wheel itself.

Wilde reached over her, closed the door. Even had someone been watching the *Sprite*, he could have seen and heard nothing. Wilde went into the living room. The woman stared at him, just rising from the table where she had been drinking coffee. She was quite striking, the pink-yellow complexion, the midnight hair, the chiselled nose and chin, the narrow eyes, hardly more than slits, the gleaming black of her pupils. So, in Holland, she might just have come from Indonesia. But he did not doubt her home was a bit north of that, which might explain a great deal. He also did not doubt that she would understand English.

'I have just killed O'Dowd,' he said. 'Do not make me shoot again.'

She settled back into her seat, each hand flat on the table, only the ripple of the heavy sweater revealing any emotion. But she wore a wedding ring. That was important. Wilde moved from the door. 'Come in here, Madeleine.'

Madeleine obeyed, and stared at the woman. There was blood on her boots. 'Oh, God,' she said. 'I have never seen a man shot before.'

'Stick around,' Wilde suggested. 'Over there.' He listened to the sound of voices, the clump of boots as Anton came on board. He moved to stand behind the woman.

The wheelhouse door opened, Anton checked, and then came on in a rush. His frame filled the doorway.

'Hold it,' Wilde said. The muzzle of the little pistol rested on the woman's neck.

'Who are you?' Anton whispered.

'Just someone who knows the score,' Wilde said. 'The whole score, Anton. So don't make any mistakes. Your wife will stay in here, with me. Get O'Dowd in here as well.'

Anton hesitated, looked at his wife, then stooped and seized Maurice O'Dowd's ankles, dragged him into the living room.

'You are the man Romain,' the Chinese woman said, softly, in French. 'And this will be Mademoiselle Corot. You see, Anton? I told you, I told O'Dowd, that we should abandon the barge. And you thought they would have to extradite him. But you are a fool, monsieur, to bother with us. Do you think we are important?'

'Only for the moment,' Wilde agreed. 'Captain, your place is on the bridge.'

Anton straightened, breathing hard. 'I cannot handle the barge by myself, into the lock.'

'Take off your sweater,' Wilde told the woman. 'Madeleine, take off your coat.' They both obeyed; the Chinese woman wore a second, lighter sweater underneath. 'Now, be a deckhand,' Wilde told Madeleine.

She stared at him for a moment, and then at the sweater, pulled it on. 'I do not know what to do.'

'When Anton is ready, he will tell you, and you'll hook those hawsers back on board. Show her where the gloves are, Anton. And when the barge enters the lock, you'll pass the hawsers back over the bollards in there. By then I'm sure Anton will be able to help you.'

Anton licked his lips. 'And afterwards?'

'You will set us ashore,' Wilde said. 'What you do with O'Dowd's body is up to you, but I should not be too public about it.'

'You will allow us to go?' Anton asked.

'As your wife has just pointed out, you are not important. You will not be able to use this route again, because we know about it. In fact, I doubt whether your employers will choose to use *you* again, now that we know about you. Perhaps it would be a good idea for you to emigrate. Just remember, if you get talking to any policemen, you will wind up serving twenty years for espionage.'

Anton hesitated, turning things over in his mind. From outside there came the blare of a loudspeaker. 'They are calling us in. You are coming, mademoiselle?'

Madeleine glanced at Wilde, followed Anton into the wheelhouse. Wilde moved round the table, remaining behind the Chinese woman. He was exhausted, the exhaustion of the anti-climax, the let-down. He knew, now, everything he had to. More than he had to. But *his* mission was complete. And it was only just after two. He could be in England for dinner. Not even Madeleine Corot was still a problem. Lucinda, for all his double talk, had only wanted this particular version of Murder Incorporated broken up without involving governments, and that was done now.

But anti-climax is a dangerous emotion, if it comes on too early. He gave the room a quick inspection. Everything one might expect to find on a barge, travelling the waterways of Western Europe. There were no weapons to be seen. Although he did not doubt that there were one or two around. There was a guitar. His, or hers? And a bookcase. But this was for show. No manifestoes, or great thoughts here; a collection of thrillers, a couple of pilot books . . . He frowned. A copy of an English *Who's Who*.

He backed over to the shelf, took out the book. He laid it on the table, so that he was facing the woman. Beneath him the engines shuddered into life, and he heard Anton shouting orders at Madeleine.

The Chinese woman gazed at the book. 'You can do nothing about that now,' she said, still speaking very softly. 'The list is already on its way to Mexico. There is another O'Dowd, monsieur, the best of the breed, and he has a photographic memory. You will not stop him, now, Mr. Romain.'

Wilde sat down, the gun pointed at her left breast. 'So this little caper is just about starting, rather than just finishing,' he said. 'I'm just trying to do my little bit, sweetheart.'

The barge moved away from the piles, the great blades of the propellers sending long shudders through the hull. So Coolidge still had a lot on his hands, in this undeclared, unseen war of attrition. But as the woman said, he could not possibly reach Robert O'Dowd, now, even if he wanted to. And Robert O'Dowd was not his target, thank God. He was finished with the O'Dowds. Thank God.

Absently he flicked the book open, riffled the pages. It was brand new, had only been opened once or twice before, he estimated. There was not a mark, inside. Well, of course, there wouldn't be.

But the woman had caught her breath, just for an instant, when he had opened the book. Now she was again breathing evenly, but she was watching him. Not a mark.

He stood the book on its spine, holding it tight shut, took his hand away. It fell open with a faint plop as the covers hit the table. The page which faced him was half-way through the L's. Light, Sir Gerald.

10

THE engines roared as Anton put them astern; the barge shuddered, and with helm hard over, swung gently against the side of the lock. Wilde raised his eyes from the book, gazed at the Chinese woman. Her expression was a mixture of watchfulness and apprehension. She could not know what he had seen, what he had deduced; there were several names beginning with L on the two pages. But she could sense that the situation had changed.

Sir Gerald, being given an injection of air, while invited to kiss the woman in the front seat. There was a thought. Only that was not Robert's way; that had been Maurice's technique. Robert believed in telling his victim, in watching them become frightened. Wilde suspected he would be disappointed in Sir Gerald's reactions. But it was still a thought. A tempting thought? No, a horrifying thought. Sir Gerald, officially, was no more than a high-ranking civil servant. So undoubtedly he had a brilliant career, could be recognised as a brilliant man. And he was one of those permanently brilliant men Madeleine had described, not dependent upon the whims of electors. Reason enough to put him on the list? Perhaps. But perhaps these people's masters knew his real occupation in life.

In any event, Gerald Light and Jonas Wilde were bound together by an umbilical cord. There could not be one without the other. Was that really relevant? Had not Gerald Light and Jonas Wilde both lived far too long? But on his trip to the United States, Gerald Light would be accompanied by his wife. Everywhere. Did they plan to assassinate Catherine as well? Wilde did not think it mattered. She was not the sort of woman to sit back and even watch her husband being kidnapped, much less killed. She knew how valuable he was. Whatever happened to Sir Gerald, it would necessarily happen to Catherine as well.

So, if Lucinda's mission was completed, Wilde's was only just beginning. If it could be done. If he could stomach what it entailed. Destruction on a scale he had not inflicted for years. Destruction of the innocent, perhaps, as well as the guilty. Of the potentially guilty as well as those with red hands.

Anton came in. 'Miss Corot works well,' he said. 'The lock is filling now. In half an hour we shall be through. In the circumstances, I shall not stop at Gouda, tonight, but will continue up the canal for a while.' He stared at Maurice O'Dowd's body. 'That will suit you, monsieur?'

'That will suit me very well,' Wilde said.

The woman said something in Chinese; Anton's gaze involuntarily flickered towards the book on the table.

'I've been reading,' Wilde said. 'Put it back for me, will you?'

So, their destruction would come first; he was willing them to action. He had promised them their lives, and so he could not kill them in cold blood. Yet he could not allow them to live, knowing that his mission was not yet completed. They could undertake nothing in the lock. Anton reached across the table, picked up the book, restored it to the shelf. Madeleine Corot stood in the doorway, taking off the heavy gloves she had used to handle the warps; she stared from one to the other, frowning. She could feel the tension.

'Yes,' Wilde said. 'To be set ashore at Boskoop would suit me right down to the ground. Because I'm afraid Miss Corot and I will have to pay a return visit to Bordeaux. Just for a while. So if you will take us to Boskoop, we can pick up a car and take a plane for Paris, eh?'

Anton said nothing. The woman's hands remained flat on the table. She watched Wilde.

'Back to Bordeaux?' Madeleine whispered. 'But that is madness, monsieur. And there is no point.'

'Because Robert will have already left? I don't think so,

mademoiselle. Do you realise that it is only half past two? Mama and Françoise will not have reached home more than an hour ago. They will not yet have made up their minds what to do.'

'But they will have by tonight. We cannot reach there again before tonight.'

'I think they may well wait to hear from Maurice,' Wilde said. 'The barges are starting their engines, Anton.'

Anton hesitated, glanced at his wife, left the room.

'Off you go, Madeleine,' Wilde said. 'There's work to be done.'

She went outside. The barge shuddered into life, the air filled with sound. The Chinese woman for the first time took her eyes from Wilde, looked to the left, through the window. Wilde watched the sweater inflating as she filled her lungs with air. She was preparing to make the first move. A woman, against a man with a gun. A professional woman.

They glided through the lock gates, engines guttering in low gear, and there was an empty bank as they joined the procession going upstream. The woman sighed. 'I may get up, monsieur?'

'Help yourself,' Wilde said.

She picked up her coffee cup, took it to the sink, washed it slowly. Her back was to him. But there was a mirror above the sink, which also served as a wash-basin. He could see her eyes, watching him, in the mirror; he could not see her hands.

Alarm bells jangled in Wilde's brain, and he hurled himself to one side. The automatic pistol peeped beneath her left armpit, the bullet struck the bulkhead immediately behind where his head had been a second earlier. All sound was lost in the roar of the engines. Real circus stuff, he thought, as he lost his balance and fell over, taking the chair with him, hitting the floor. For the moment he was shielded by the table, could see only her legs. But these immediately folded as she hit the deck, the pistol thrust forward, her magnificent face impassive, but her deep eyes alive with the

bloodlust. What she did not know about guns, and how to
use them, would not fill a corner of a postage stamp. But
there were too many odds against her. He had already fired
twice, hitting her legs each time; now he fired again, at her
body, as she struck the deck. Then he was on his feet again,
moving round the table. For she continued firing, three
times, sightlessly and without aim, now, the reflex action
of a mind as hate-filled as his own.

Lucinda's piece of cake. Wilde stood above her, looked
down at the cloud of black hair obscuring her face, at the
red liquid seeping out from under the sweater, turned to the
door as Anton burst through. Now the whole afternoon was
tinged with the red edge of hatred. Hatred of the men who
dreamed of world domination, who thought of human lives
only as kindling for their particular fires; hatred of the men
who felt it necessary to oppose them; hatred of life itself,
for being the greatest predator of them all. Hatred which
would carry him through, now. Through and beyond. Which
would welcome death at any moment. But which, until
then, would spit death itself, time and again, until there
was no enemy left.

So Anton never had a chance. He checked at the sight
of the gun in Wilde's hand, the muzzle moving up on his
body, smiled when Wilde squeezed and there was an aim-
less click, grinned as he moved forward. Wilde dropped
the gun, caught Anton's swinging right hand in his left fist,
closed his fingers and swung the big man round. Anton
gasped, and the grin faded. In that split second he knew
that the gun had not been relevant. Before he could decide
why, he had hit the table, sagging like a sack of coal, bounc-
ing on the deck, eyes and mouth open, life already ended.

From behind him, Madeleine screamed. The barge was
already swinging off the straight, making for the bank. Wilde
knocked the girl aside with a swing of his hand, reached the
wheel, put the helm hard to starboard and the engine astern.
How slowly the huge craft turned. How slowly, and how
ineffectively. The bow was round, but the sideways movement continued, and was a scraping crunch as the steel hull

struck the wooden breakwaters on the side of the canal, splintering them and driving onwards into the earth of the bank. Wilde thrust the engine ahead, just for a moment, spun the wheel to port to bring the bows back, jammed the gear lever into neutral, and ran on deck. For the moment the barge was stationary. 'Get that bow warp,' he shouted at Madeleine, and she went stumbling along the deck, falling to her hands and knees and regaining her feet, the heavy rope in her hands.

Wilde seized the stern hawser, took a flying leap to the shore. He dragged the warp up the bank, passed it round a tree-trunk, looped it back on itself and tied a gigantic bowline, ran along the bank. Madeleine was standing in the bow, the hawser in her hands, her back to the shore, gazing in utter horror at another barge, the last out of the lock, nosing in alongside them.

'What has happened?' the bargee called, leaning out of his wheelhouse.

Wilde made the bow warp fast. 'The steering gear has parted,' he said. 'It is nothing serious.' He regained the deck, went aft.

The bargee watched him for a moment, while the barge gradually lost way, some twelve feet away from the *Sprite*. 'Where is Anton?'

'Below,' Wilde explained. 'Mending the steering. There is nothing to worry about, he says. We shall soon be under way again.'

'You are Mr. O'Dowd?' the bargee asked.

'That's me,' Wilde agreed. 'Maurice O'Dowd. Why, did Anton tell you I was joining him?'

'He said something about a friend, back at the lock.' The bargee nodded to himself. 'Anton is good, with engines.' He waved his hand, stepped back into the wheelhouse, and the barge moved away.

Madeleine sat on the hatch cover, wiped sweat and snow from her brow. 'Oh, my God,' she said. 'Suppose he had come ashore?'

'He didn't.' Wilde went into the living quarters, drew the curtains, locked the door on the three bodies.

'What does it matter?' Madeleine asked. 'They must be found, eventually.'

'Eventually,' Wilde said.

'Soon; this is not a usual place for a barge to be tied up.'

'So we'll hurry.' He stepped ashore, held out his hands for her. She hesitated, then jumped into his arms, and he set her on the bank. There was a barge coming downstream now. Once again the wheelhouse door opened, and the bargee came on deck. Wilde waved, got a wave in return, and the barge continued on its way. 'Maybe sooner. So let's hurry. There's the railway bridge; the car will be just through those trees.'

She panted at his side. 'What can you hope to accomplish, monsieur? It is two hours to Amsterdam by car, an hour to Paris by plane, and another two hours to Bordeaux, by plane. Even if everything goes according to plan, and no one tries to stop us. At the very least that is half past seven tonight.'

Tonight being . . . still Thursday. How easy it was to lose track. 'Seven-thirty tonight will be time enough,' he said, and saw the car, gleaming quietly amidst the trees.

'But Robert will have already left,' she wailed.

Wilde opened the door and thrust her in. 'Maybe not. Tell me, sweetheart, when we had our set-to, a few moments back, supposing you'd got that knife into my gut, what would you have done next? Apart from being violently sick.'

She flushed. 'I don't know.'

'Oh yes, you do, darling. You must have had some plan. Why kill me at all? You've been promised asylum. You thought that if you killed me, that would prove you couldn't have written those letters, and Robert would have had to take you back.'

She shrugged. 'I suppose so, monsieur. Something like that.'

'So, imagine me lying dead over there. What would you

have done next? Tried to contact Robert? Or Maurice?'
'Oh, Robert, monsieur. But it doesn't . . .'
He reversed the car, headed it up the bumpy track towards
the motorway. 'How would you contact Robert? You'd
want to do it in a hurry.'
'Well,' she said. 'I suppose I would telephone, monsieur,
in the hopes of catching him before he left.'
'Do you know,' Wilde said. 'I think that's a good idea.
We'll find a phone in Boskoop.'

(ii)

She shivered, all the time. They leaned against each other,
their cheeks pressed together. Wilde had written what he
wanted her to say, on the back of the road map supplied
with the car. But he kept his hands close to her throat.
'Dort?' asked the bored girl on the exchange. 'Where is
that, fräulein?'
'In France,' Madeleine explained. 'In the Departmente
Gironde. There are only two numbers in the village.'
'Well, hold on, fräulein. I will see if we can get through.'
Madeleine rested the receiver on top of the box, leaned
against Wilde. 'It will do no good, monsieur. Robert knows
me too well. He will know, from my voice . . . and what does
it matter now? You have killed Maurice and Jack. You
have destroyed the O'Dowds.'
'Not yet,' Wilde said. 'Not sufficiently. And you want to
remember, mademoiselle, that I am your only hope of sur-
vival. More than that, I am also your executioner, should
you make a single mistake.'
There were clicks from the line. 'I have your call, fräulein.'
There was a lot of money to be put in the slot. But Wilde
had collected change at his lunchtime restaurant.
'Hello? Hello, who is there?'
'Aimee?' Madeleine gasped for breath. 'Is Monsieur
Robert there, Aimee?'

'Oh yes, mademoiselle. Mademoiselle Madeleine, is it? Oh yes, mademoiselle. The family is just lunching.'

Wilde almost smiled. The O'Dowds, sitting down to lunch, within hours of Jack's death, with catastrophe hanging over them.

'I would like to speak to Monsieur Robert,' Madeleine said.

'I will call him, mademoiselle.' There was a clang as Aimee laid down the receiver. Madeleine stared at Wilde with horror-stricken eyes. He fed the meter, moved closer. One hand rested on her throat.

'Madeleine?' Robert's turn to be breathless. 'Where are you?'

'I am in Holland. Robert. Robert, darling. Listen to me. Romain. The man Romain. He has *gone away*. He will not trouble you again.' The words came out in a tumbling rush. Wilde's fingers beat a tattoo on her throat.

There was a brief silence.

'You are sure of this?' Robert O'Dowd asked at last.

'I saw him off myself,' she said. 'He wished to find Maurice again, and so he made me bring him to Holland. But before we reached Maurice, I persuaded him to leave things as they were, and go away. I did that, Robert.'

Again the hesitation. Wilde fed the meter.

'His friends will be sorry he left so abruptly,' Robert said.

'His friends do not know he has gone, Robert. They will not know, for some time. They cannot go. Robert. Listen to me. I made him leave, Robert. After everything that has happened, *I* made him leave. I did not write those letters, Robert. You must know I did not write them, now.'

This time the silence was longer.

'Yes,' Robert said at last. 'Yes, I understand. Have you seen Maurice?'

She stared at Wilde, her eyes wide. He shook his head.

'No,' she said. 'No, Robert. I thought it best not to. I wished to tell you first. I wanted you to understand. Robert. I want to come down to Dort. I must see you, Robert.

It is terribly important. Romain talked to me. He did a lot
of talking. All the way from Paris to Amsterdam. I must
see you, Robert. I can catch a plane from Amsterdam to
Paris, and another for Bordeaux.'

'It is snowing,' Robert said. 'I think the airport is closed.'

'I will get there,' Madeleine said. 'I promise. Please . . .
do nothing until you see me, Robert.'

'Yes,' Robert said. 'It would be a good idea for you to
leave Holland, Madeleine. Quickly. I will look forward to
seeing you. And, Madeleine . . . I am sorry for what happened last night. It would not have happened had I been
there.'

'I know,' she said. 'I know. Robert . . .'

Wilde's hand closed on her throat.

'Madeleine?' Robert asked. 'Madeleine? Are you there?'

Wilde's fingers slackened. Madeleine gasped for breath.
'Yes. It was nothing. A frog in my throat. I will hang up
now, and go to the airport. I will see you, if not tonight, first
thing tomorrow.'

She replaced the receiver.

'You did that very well,' Wilde said.

She stared at him. 'But if I did not write those letters,
monsieur, who did? Who *could* have done such a thing?'

'I imagine,' Wilde said, 'that Robert is about to do a bit of
brooding on that subject as well.'

(iii)

Paris was clear. But it was six o'clock when they landed, and
as Robert O'Dowd had suggested, Bordeaux airport was
closed. But Wilde had already decided that he would drive
if he had to; unless he was very unlucky with the weather,
he should make Bordeaux by two in the morning. That should
be sufficient. That *should* be sufficient.

He hired a Renault. The girl stared at him, and then at
Madeleine. No doubt with reason. There was dirt on his

trousers, and his raincoat was torn. There was dirt on Madeleine's tights, and on her coat as well. People remembered things like that. But they would remember the dirt more than the face.

Far more important was exactly what Madeleine now thought about everything. She had not spoken a word since leaving Boskoop, and this time she had not asked for cigarettes. She had talked herself out this morning, and since then, her ideas on Wilde himself had changed. She was afraid of *him* now, where before she had only been afraid of what he stood for. And she was afraid of Robert, too, now, because of that telephone call. When the two men eventually met, she would be in the middle. She had to choose, finally, and correctly. But he did not think she had much choice left now; Robert would never trust her again, after she showed up with Jules Romain. The only risk lay in how genuinely in love with him she was. Perhaps because, up to this moment, he had never been on the receiving end of such a love, he could not be sure of what might happen. For one of the very few occasions in recent years, he was operating outside of his experience. He could only wait, and go on, to the end, and hope he made it. He was cutting things very fine. Far too fine. He looked at his watch; Sammy Bennett would be having dinner, and thinking about leaving Bordeaux, for the battle against the tide down to Dort.

He swung through Longjumeau to pick up the N20. The road itself had been cleared, but there was snow on the pavements and the rooftops, and it seemed to grow colder every moment; once when he blinked, the car drifted across the street, which was, fortunately, at that moment empty.

Here was the biggest of all his problems. The last sleep he had had had been on Tuesday night, and he still carried a hangover from last night. His mind felt disorientated; he seemed to have been driving a car or sitting in an aircraft for all of his life. So, his reactions were slowed down, his system was existing entirely on hatred. Hatred, and the thought of Catherine, seated in the back of a car, while some courteous gentleman pushed up the sleeve and introduced a needle into that Riviera complexion. What would they offer Catherine, to keep her happy, while she died?

But fatigue was gnawing even at the borders of his hatred. He glanced at the woman. 'How do you feel?'

She raised her head. 'I do not feel, monsieur. Not now.'

He changed down, allowed the car to drift to a stop at the roadside. 'Then drive.'

It was a risk, but less of one, he estimated, than the risk of his crashing the car. 'No tricks now,' he said.

She crawled over him, unbuttoned her coat, sent the car roaring into the night. Presumably she was as tired as he. But she drove well. Of course. This was her professional position in the organisation. Driving executioners to their victims. Quite like old times.

'You have no gun now,' she said, half to herself. 'How will you kill him? You think you will break his neck, as you broke Jack's neck?'

'I'll play it by ear.'

'Robert is not like his brothers, monsieur,' she said. 'You will not find it so easy, with him. Believe me.'

'I do,' Wilde said.

'But you will persist. This affair has taken on a madness. You are determined to kill, and kill, and kill, like a wild animal . . .'

'Isn't that what you have been doing these past couple of years?'

'People who deserved to die.'

'For being American citizens?' There's a condemnation. Did I ever tell you that my old lady was a New England miss? Now shut up, and keep your eyes on the road.'

She subsided into silence, and they droned into the night. Close beside the road a train screamed along the track to Orléans, a long snake of light, carrying its passengers home to Christmas. A happy train.

Orléans was busy, and they were slowed to a crawl. It took them half an hour to pick up the N152 for Tours, and

by now it was snowing again. Wilde rolled his window down
to allow the cold air on to his face. Twice he had nearly
dozed off, and he figured Madeleine would only let him do it
once. How simple it would be just to make her pull into the
side of the road, and leave her body in a ditch. Robert
O'Dowd would do that.

Now they were in the valley of the Loire; the river rustled
by to the left of the road. Suddenly the car checked, turning
into the side of the road, gliding to a halt. Wilde sat up.
'Petrol?'

Madeleine Corot left her hands on the wheel, stared into
the darkness; she had switched off the lights.

'Sweetheart,' Wilde said. 'We still have a long way to go,
and it's already nine o'clock.'

'Monsieur,' she said. 'There is no need for you to return
to Dort. As an organisation, the O'Dowds will never function again. Mama has now lost three sons. She will not per-
mit it to function again. She said as much last night, in the
apartment. And with Anton dead as well . . .'

'So you weren't quite so tight as you seemed,' Wilde said.
'Last night. As a matter of fact, I agree with you, mademoiselle. I don't think they will ever function again, in this
part of the world. But Robert is committed to getting a new
group going, in Mexico.'

'That is no concern of yours, monsieur. At least, it is not a
sufficient reason for taking a man's life, for risking your own.
I do not know who you work for, but it is certainly a
government, whether British or America. You can tell them
what has happened, everything you have learned. Let them
take the necessary steps to protect their people. I will tell them
for you, if you wish.'

'You?'

'If you wish.' Her fingers were right on the steering wheel.
'Or I will do anything else you wish, monsieur.' Still she
gazed into the darkness. 'They say . . .' She sucked air into
her lungs. 'I have been told that I am beautiful, monsieur.'

'They weren't lying, Madeleine.'

'I am also faithful, monsieur. I am still, in my heart, faithful to Robert, because he once gave me his love. I think perhaps he lied on the telephone. I think perhaps he would have acted exactly as his mother did. Yet am I reluctant to see him die.'

'Just now you were saying that it wouldn't be easy.'

She shrugged. 'Not easy, monsieur. But I do not think you are an easy man. I do not want him to die, monsieur. In exchange for his life, I would give my faithfulness to you. I do not lie, monsieur. I . . . I have not a passionate nature. With Robert I could feel passion, but even then, rarely. For you, monsieur, in exchange for his life, I would feel passion. I would throw away my beliefs, my inhibitions. I can see passion in everything you do. In the way you look at people. In the way you breathe. I would match your passion, monsieur, if you wished it.' She turned, violently, seized his hands, guided them to her breasts. The cold had reached her nipples, and even under the dress they were enormous. How strange, he thought, that these are breasts I have never seen. In his amoral world, feminine modesty was unknown, except here in this strange, confused, tragic woman, who now offered herself to him. Because once again he believed her. He did not think she had ever told a lie before today. He did not think she knew how. How different would everything have been could the O'Dowds, who surely knew her so much better than he did, have made themselves believe that simple little truth.

And how tragic that, in her innocence, as a woman, her attempts to seduce him were so similar to the puppy love of Françoise.

Gently he withdrew his hands. 'I have a one-track mind, Madeleine.'

Her face was a blur in the darkness. 'And there is another woman. One you can trust, and love. One who feels passion.'

'Sometimes,' he said. 'Sometimes, there is another woman. Now, will you drive, or will I?'

(iv)

They filled with petrol in Tours, and he took the wheel again. Perhaps she slept. She had not spoken another word. How well could you come to know someone in forty-eight hours? Forty-eight hours in which you had killed together. How strange that he had only kissed this girl once, while she had tried to drive a knife into his ribs, and yet he felt he knew her more intimately than he knew Catherine Light.

The snow stopped beyond Tours, but it remained dusted on the road, made driving treacherous. At least it kept him awake. But time was passing. Sammy Bennett would be forcing his way downriver, peering into the snow and cursing. He'd reach Dort at four. Would he wait? Dare he wait? And if Wilde did not get there until after four, what then? There was slowly building up a hornet's nest, all looking for the man Jules Romain. It would take time for the Paris police to work out what had happened in the O'Dowd flat; they could never be sure. The Dutch police would have no more than a description, to start with. But it would be a double description, of a man and a woman, travelling together; they would trace the couple to Schipfol, and from there to Paris, and from Orly in a hired car. There they would lose them, for a moment, but following a murder in Dort, by a man answering the same description . . . even if Jules Romain and Madeleine Corot were by then on a plane for England, the police would be waiting for them. Jules Romain had to disappear in Dort, to have any hope of survival. And Jules Romain's disappearance depended on Sammy Bennett.

But it was three o'clock when they raced across the bridge below Bordeaux, leaving the city, silent and snow-swept, on their left. Wilde took the corner at the southern end of the bridge on two wheels, sent them into a long skid which brought Madeleine upright, both hands to her throat. Still she did not speak, and now he had the car racing down the lonely road, through Pauillac, silent although still illuminated by its eternal flame, and then the deserted, shuttered village of Dort. Three-thirty. Half an hour. Half an hour, to commit murder, successfully, and get out again.

He turned left, into the drive, doused his lights. It was utterly dark, but the even deeper tree shadows to either side guided him up the drive. And before him, to his surprise, the house was a blaze of light. At half past three in the morning? Robert O'Dowd was expecting guests.

Madeleine was sitting up now, her hands clenched together. 'He knows, monsieur,' she whispered. 'He knows.'

'If he does, he's psychic.' Wilde braked, looked at his watch again. Three-forty. Only twenty minutes. No time to play around, to practise finesse, to reconnoitre. To be stuck in Dort was to be finished, anyway. But wasn't this what he wanted? Hadn't he always been quite sure that Robert O'Dowd would mean the end? He opened his door. 'Come on, sweetheart.'

'You wish me to come, monsieur?'

'I'm not all that keen on leaving you on your own, Madeleine, and it's just possible that I may need you. But do try to remember, there's only me now, for you, in the whole wide world.'

She got out of the car, buttoned her coat. He urged her to the wide steps, up them to the patio. Before them the house seemed to grow in size, light belching from every window, looming over the patio. There was no shelter, and there could be ten, twenty people watching them. But there could only be four O'Dowds here now.

'Do you know these dogs?' Wilde asked. 'Or, perhaps, I should say, do they know you?'

'Yes, monsieur.'

'I'm glad to hear it. Convince them.'

The front door stood open, and the dogs, Soult and Ney, came scampering up the hallway, barking and howling, stopping when they saw Madeleine. 'Good dogs,' she said. 'Good dogs. Good Ney. Good Soult. Mr. Romain, why should this door be open, and every light on? I am afraid.'

'So am I,' Wilde said. 'I'm afraid they may have cleared
off despite your call. The whole lot of them.' He stepped
inside. But they would not have gone, and left their dogs.
The skin on his neck crawled, and the short hairs seemed to
stand erect. It was a very long time since he had known anything so close to physical fear. But to stand in this hallway,
in a house surely dedicated to his destruction, was a dis-
tressing experience. 'Come on.' He held her hand, turned
to the left, into the dining room. The family had eaten dinner, several hours ago, but the table had not been cleared.
Four places, four plates, four half-consumed bottles of wine.
He went for the inner staircase, still dragging Madeleine
behind him, ran up the steps into the drawing room, checked,
every muscle tensed, his pounding heart settling away to
an even beat as he realised his quest was at an end.

Robert O'Dowd sat facing the stairs, in a comfortable
armchair. His head leaned back against the upholstery, he
looked relaxed, at ease; there was even a half-smile on his
face. But Robert O'Dowd was dead.

Madeleine freed her hand, ran forward, knelt at his side.
Wilde stood beside her, stooped, picked up the syringe
which had fallen from his fingers to the floor.

'A suitable way to die, do you not think?' asked Charles
O'Dowd. He stood in the doorway, leaning on a stick. 'In
view of the way he so often killed.'

Wilde turned to face him. His muscles were still tensed,
the surges of murderous energy were still coursing through
his arteries. But already he knew that his mission was fin-
ised. It had finished several hours ago, the moment Robert
O'Dowd had understood that Madeleine Corot had not
written the two letters.

'He has been dead for three hours, Mr. Romain,' Charles
O'Dowd said. 'I have telephoned our family doctor in Bor-
deaux, but he is out on a call. He will be here, eventually.
He will agree with me, that it must have been a heart attack.
How tragic, to lose two sons on consecutive days.'

'Not two, Mr. O'Dowd,' Wilde said. 'Three. I am truly sorry.'

Charles O'Dowd sighed. 'But it was your job, eh? Oh, yes. I did not intend this, Mr. Romain. I did not intend this. But what does any human being intend? How *can* he intend, when so much is at the mercy of fate?' Charles O'Dowd sat down. 'All this, for nothing. For nothing but death. How much better to go gracefully bankrupt. I wanted to. I would not have been destitute. I could have sold the house, you know, Mr. Romain. I would have got a good price. But they would not hear of it. And when I knew what they were intending, I warned them. They ignored me. And I did nothing about it, as they knew would be the case. They were my own children. Until they executed my son. They executed their own brother. She executed her own son. For being a failure. It was then I knew that they were not human, Mr. Romain. No longer human. That I had married a monster, and thereby fathered a brood of monsters. But I only meant to restrain, not destroy them, all.'

'Where is Mrs. O'Dowd?'

Charles O'Dowd raised his head. 'In her room, Mr. Romain. Oh, she is human enough to weep for Robert. He was her favourite. She cannot harm you, or your government now.'

'I know that, Mr. O'Dowd. And Françoise?'

'She also weeps, Mr. Romain. You should know that she can weep.'

'She is not like her brothers, Mr. O'Dowd,' Wilde said. 'Be sure she does not change.' He took Madeleine's hand— she had remained staring at her dead lover—pulled her to the stairs, hurried her down. The dogs lay by the front door, gazed at them silently. They got into the car, Wilde reversed it, drove into Dort.

'You knew,' she whispered. 'You knew it was Papa who wrote those letters.'

'It seemed reasonable, by a process of elimination. And I knew something else, that Charles O'Dowd was the only creature in this world who Robert loved. Sad, but true.'

'So if it came to a point where he had to destroy his father, he preferred to destroy himself. Oh, God, monsieur. What is going to become of us all?'

'You and I,' Wilde said, 'are about to incur a bad case of chilblains.' He helped her out of the car, took her on to the dock. The time was three minutes to four, and a converted M.F.V. came nosing out of the darkness, rattled alongside. A man stepped ashore with a warp, but Wilde was already on board, assisting Madeleine on to the deck. The wheel-house door opened, and Sammy Bennett, short, thick-shouldered, crag-faced, looking like a Himalayan bear in his oilskins, worn over several heavy sweaters, peered at them.

'Dead on time,' he said. 'And with a blonde. Christ Almighty. Just like Coolidge said. A piece of cake. A bloody piece of cake. You know something, Jonas; you have the luck of the Irish.'

(v)

There was no party tonight. But Betty mixed daiquiris. 'I won't say happy Christmas,' she said. 'But I'm having a New Year's get together tomorrow. Care to come?'

'Quite a tale,' Lucinda remarked. 'Quite an operation. I apologise, Jonas. I had no idea it would be so big.'

'Neither did I,' Wilde agreed.

Lucinda jerked a thumb at the newspapers lying on the coffee table. 'Still, you seem to have got away with it. The Dutch police are going wild about their problems, but they haven't linked their man with the chap who wandered off after the fire in Auteuil; there's no reason why they should. The French police *have* linked him with the blonde Mademoiselle Corot, and with the abandoned car in Dort, but they're assuming he was making for Spain. That bother you?'

'Not *me*. They've almost no facial description at all.'

'Yeah. And the British police have taken a look at Dort, I understand, and come to the conclusion that's the end of the line. Which just about sums it up. So you'll be back off to your boat in the sun, I guess. Does Sir Gerald know you're in England?'

'Not unless you've told him.'

'I haven't.'

'Then let's leave it like that.'

'Yeah. It just so happens, Jonas, that I may have to come looking for you again. As your playmate said, we're already fighting world war three. And until they dispose of enough ICBMs to take us on face to face, it's going to be fought this way. You're worth a regiment.'

Wilde finished his daiquiri.

'What gets me,' Lucinda said, 'is how they recruited these people, in the first place. Granted the anti-British, anti-American, nihilistic philosophy, there had to be something more.'

'There was,' Wilde said. 'Oidium.'

'Come again?'

'It's a disease which hits the wine crop. Basically mildew. It ruins both the colour and the quality of the wine. The affected grapes should be scrapped. In the O'Dowds' case, four years ago, this meant the entire crop, and as they'd just finished virtually rebuilding that house of theirs, that would have meant bankruptcy. Old Charles would have been willing to sell up, but the boys and Mama wouldn't let him; O'Dowds had lived in Dort for three hundred years. I think what really tempted them was that they had already contracted to ship a large part of that year's wine to the Far East, and they figured, what the hell, no one out there will know the difference. But they made a mistake; someone did know the difference. Well, you know what those characters can do with a blonde in the bedroom; here they had several thousand barrels of dud wine, shipped by a name grower, and those big French growers are as proud of their reputations as diamond merchants. There was money involved, too; I suspect their new masters financed the replanting, because I gather things were a bit tight right then. Presumably there was also a bit of brain washing involved; Robert was forced to spend four months learning his new trade.'

'Now, just how did you find the time to find about their business problems?' Lucinda asked.

'I like claret, remember? And Château Dort has always been one of my favourites. The trouble with replanting, you see, is that you change the character of the wine. Not all that much, maybe, so long as you use the same type of grape, but enough to notice. O'Dowd gave me some of the current crop, and it's quite different to the old Dort. After that, it was just a matter of relating all the little oddities I'd noticed. So now, you tell me, what have you done with Miss Corot?'

'She's a funny kid,' Lucinda said. 'I'm employing her in my section, as a matter of fact. For the time being. She'll need a lot of re-education, but she could turn out all right.'

'And if she won't re-educate? I promised her asylum.'

'We'll cross that bridge when we come to it. Well, I've got to get along.' He stood up. 'You know, you were only paid for one, and you did three; that telephone call was as lethal as any bullet. I figure you deserve a bonus.'

'Forget it,' Wilde said. 'Betty can make me a few more daiquiris. Although, come to think of it, Coolidge, there is something you can do for me. Two things.'

'Shoot.'

'I want you to get two of the largest bunches of roses you can lay hands on, one white, the other red. The white are to go to Françoise O'Dowd.'

'Fair enough. And the red?'

'Come Sunday, which is the day after tomorrow, remember, you have one of your boys take the red to the street next to the O'Dowd Paris flat. At the end of the street there's a little fountain. He's to leave them at the foot of the fountain. Sunday, mind. And he must be there and gone by noon.'

'Consider it done. I'll be in touch.'

The door closed. Betty mixed a fresh batch of daiquiris. 'So who is *that* one?' she asked.

'Do you know, I never found out.' Wilde lit a Belfleur cigar. 'But I'm an optimist.'